camera

Originally published in French as *L'appareil-photo* by
Les Editions de Minuit, 1988

First English translation, 2008

Library of Congress Cataloging-in-Publication Data

Toussaint, Jean-Philippe.
[Appareil-photo. English]
Camera / Jean-Philippe Toussaint ; translation by Matthew B. Smith.
p. cm.
ISBN 978-1-56478-522-0 (alk. paper)
I. Smith, Matthew B. II. Title.
PQ2680.O86A8713 2008
843'.914--dc22

2008012294

Partially funded by a grant from the Illinois Arts Council, a state Agency, and by the University of Illinois at Urbana-Champaign

This work has been published, in part, thanks to the French Ministry of Culture—National Book Center

www.dalkeyarchive.com

Printed on permanent/durable acid-free paper and bound in the United States of America

jean-philippe toussaint

camera

translated from the French by Matthew B. Smith

Dalkey Archive Press • Champaign and London

It was at about the same time in my life, a calm life in which ordinarily nothing happened, that two events coincided, events that, taken separately, were of hardly any interest, and that, considered together, were unfortunately not connected in any way. As it happens I had just decided to learn how to drive, and I had barely begun to get used to this idea when some news reached me by mail: a long-lost friend, in a letter composed with a type writer, a rather old type writer, had informed me he was getting married. Now, personally, if there's one thing that terrifies me, it's long-lost friends.

Thus, one morning, I went to look into taking driving classes at the driver's ed office. It was a rather large place, almost dark, in the back of which several rows of chairs were arranged in front of a projection screen. The walls were covered with all sorts of street signs, and some pale blue notices here and there, faded and dated. The young lady who helped me gave me a list of documents that I had to provide in order to sign up for the course, informed me of the cost and the number of classes I would have to take, a maximum of a dozen for the permit, twenty for the license, if everything went well. Then, opening a drawer, she handed me a paper to fill out, which I pushed back towards her without even glancing at, explaining to her that there wasn't any rush, I'd prefer to fill it out later, if that was possible, when I'd come back with all the documents, that seemed much easier to me.

I then spent the day at my place, read the newspaper, went through some of my mail. Towards evening, it happened by chance that I passed by the driver's ed office again. I seized the opportunity to push open the door, and the young lady, seeing me come in, thought that, in fact, I had come back to sign up for the course. I had to inform her that this was not the case, letting her believe that the process was coming along; I already had a photocopy of my passport and I was planning to find out before too long how I should go about obtaining my birth certificate. She gave me a perplexed look and reminded me on my way out not to forget the photos (right, right, I said, four photos).

That same night, having obtained my birth certificate (I even had a copy made), I went back to the driver's ed office. I paused for a second at the threshold of the door and raised my head towards a sonorous device, a copper bell being tapped by a little hammer. Smiling, the young lady explained to me that usually she unplugged it when she was there, and, getting up, she walked out from behind her desk, wearing a thin, light-colored frock, and crossed the room to show me what triggered the bell. It was a rather ingenious system, I must say, and we enjoyed ourselves for a few minutes playing with it, cutting off then putting back on the sound, opening and shutting the door, at times from the inside and at others from the outside, and then it started to get dark. We were outside still playing with the apparatus when the phone rang. She went to answer it and, while she was talking, I waited next to her, slightly moving objects on her desk, opening random drawers. Once she had hung up, she asked me how my application was coming along, and together we made a sort of inventory of all the documents I had already gotten together. It seemed to me that, in order to be able to turn in the application, the only things that were missing, apart from the self-addressed envelope, were the photos. Before leaving, I let her know that, speaking of photos, a little while ago, at my house, I had found some photos of myself when I was little. Why don't I show them to you, I said while taking out the envelope from my coat pocket, and, walking around to the other side of her desk, I went through them one by one, leaning over her shoulder in order to point to what I was explaining. So, there, I said, I'm standing next to my father, and there, that's my sister in my mom's arms. There, we're both with my sister in the pool; behind the mud, that's my sister all right, so little. There, that's us again, my sister and I, in the pool. There you have it, I said, putting the photos back into the envelope, I think you'll agree that this is of little use to us—for the application—I said.

When, the next morning, I showed up at the driver's ed office as soon as it opened (I still didn't have the photos, it wasn't even worth asking), the young lady was busy making tea on a little burner. She was wearing a large white woolen sweater over her dress, and looked sleepy. I went to sit down on a chair facing the projection screen and, unfolding my newspaper, started reading it so as not to inconvenience her. We made small talk while I was catching up with current events and, when her tea was ready, she asked me, yawning, if I would like a cup. Without putting down the paper, still reading, I told her no, God forbid, what's the world coming to? But a cup of coffee, on the other hand, I said, putting down the paper, I wouldn't turn down. Even some Nescafé, I said. While the young lady went to get some Nescafé (grab some croissants too, I said, while you're up), I waited alone in the office and, so as not to be bothered, I padlocked the glass door. I picked up reading where I had left off when I heard some cute little knocks behind me at the door. I looked up, saddened, and turned around to see that it wasn't the young lady, but a young man, an unattractive one at that, wearing a sort of green raincoat and loafers with white socks. I put my paper down again and got up to open the door—this guy was going to get it. What do you want? I asked. I just turned eighteen, he said (as if he was trying to impress me). We're closed, I said. But I was already here yesterday, he added, I just wanted to drop off my application. Let's not be stubborn, I said, slowly closing my eyes. I shut the door. Then, while he walked away, I stayed behind the window for a couple of minutes, hands in coat pockets, looking at the view, pensive. Birds were pecking at crumbs on the sidewalk. The young man, a little further out, had reached his moped and was busy trying to secure his bag to his bike with the help of frayed bungee cords. He turned around to glance in my direction and, getting on his moped, rode off trailing a bus, it's hopeless, now get going. During breakfast, which we, the young lady and I, had together a little while later in front of the projection screen, having placed a chair in front of us and torn open the longer part of the croissant bag, we chatted about this and that, trying to get to know each other a little bit better. Sitting next to me, legs crossed, she had rolled up the sleeves of her big sweater and was massaging her arm nonchalantly, head lowered, still looking sleepy. We talked about everything and nothing, casually, taking a slow sip from time to time. Then, while she started to clean up our mess, I picked all the scattered crumbs off the chair and, asking me what I was planning on doing today, I told her that I was probably going to try to get the photos taken care of. She sat back down behind her desk and, busy sorting through some papers, told me, yawning, that at this pace I would never finish my application. Personally, I didn't completely agree. She misunderstood my method, in my opinion, not realizing that my approach, rather obscure to those unfamiliar, was based on the idea that in my struggle with reality, I could exhaust any opponent with whom I was grappling, like one can wear out an olive, for example, before successfully stabbing it with a fork, and that my propensity not to hasten matters, far from having a negative effect, in fact prepared for me a fertile ground where, when things seemed ripe, I could make my move with ease.

The morning calmly passed. Around eleven o'clock, we went to pick up the young lady's son at school. Little Pierre, whom she had with her first husband—she explained this to me while we drove to the school in her big Volvo—had been very affected by their divorce (yes, yes, I can imagine), but he was doing really well in school now, he got A's in every subject, in math, in gym class. We were moving very fast and, sitting next to her in the Volvo, I was looking at her out of the corner of my eye, fascinated by the contrast between the prodigious speed at which she was driving and the delightful, sleepy look that she still had, her little eyes on the verge of closing behind her glasses. And in art too, she added yawing, in art. And in art too, I said. Of course, she assured me, almost angry at the idea that I could even doubt the exceptional capabilities of little Pierre. He was going to be fluent in many languages by the time he was older, my little Pierre, she was saying, at least in English and in Japanese (she was adamant about Japanese), it's an important language for the future, Japanese. In thirty years everyone will speak Japanese. Oh, really? In business, she clarified, yawning (she was adorable), in business. Little Pierre would be a businessman, a writer, an economist, a diplomat. Wearing a red snow-jacket and a balaclava hat, we looked at him tenderly, waiting behind the school gate. Next to us, on the sidewalk, standing apart, a small group of mothers who seemed to have known each other for a long time were chatting informally. We went through the gate and I stayed next to the door, letting the young lady work her way through the playground. I didn't feel very comfortable in there because I didn't know anyone, and I dawdled alongside the gate, acting casual, while the young lady conversed with Little Pierre's teacher next to the school entrance. I ended up joining them, and the teacher, while continuing to speak, gave me a look to acknowledge my presence and I nodded back to her, folding my arms across my chest. She talked to us about how he was doing in school, little Pierre, who was very bright in certain subjects, she said, but not always well-behaved in class, she was sorry to have to tell us, and, suddenly, judging that these words would be better understood by the father, she continued to speak turning her attention towards me, and I listened attentively, nodding my head (yes, yes, I understand, I said, I understand), admitting that one bad apple can spoil the whole barrel.

In the following days, I had to make a quick trip to Milan. I spent two interminable days there, if I remember correctly, in which, between two meetings, I occupied my time searching the city for English and French newspapers, which I read more or less fully in various parks, moving from one bench to the next in order to follow the progression of the sun. A ray of light flickered and pleasantly tickled my nostril while I leafed peacefully through the paper, sneezing on my bench, my allergies acting up from this blissful contact with the first rays of sunlight. Besides that, having nothing special to do in Milan—read the paper, of course, lifting my head from time to time to contemplate the shaded pathways of the park—I walked around almost the whole day, going from place to place with my newspapers under my arm, and was soon inconvenienced by numerous little annoying blisters that were perniciously forming between my toes (right there where my baby skin is so delicate, let it be a warning to you). It got to the point where I began walking in an unnatural way, to say the least, stiff and grimacing, and I found myself rather discomforted all in all, removing my shoe and my sock as soon as I stopped at a crosswalk in order to check out the damage that had been done. When the crosswalk sign turned green, rather than springing forward to skip across the road, balancing on one leg I put my sock back on and, on the verge of falling, hopping in place on the sidewalk to keep my balance, I realized that I was in the presence of one of my hosts in Milan, Il Signore Gambini, the same man who came to the airport two nights ago to welcome me and drive me to the hotel. A charming man, to say the least, who, the night of my arrival, after showing me to my room, had invited me to have a whiskey with him at the hotel's international bar, so as to give me various documents for work, as well as a map of the city printed in a small brochure that he had meticulously annotated in order to facilitate my visits to different museums in the city, and who, still there, while I was straining to put back on my shoe, asked me with the utmost amiability and with a look of concern if he could help me with anything (a pedicure, oh yes, I exclaimed grabbing his arm).

The beautician's where Il Signore Gambini led me (we traveled by taxi) was a building of great elegance, where customers were treated in small, individual rooms lining an opulent lounge that served as a waiting room and where, around a coffee table topped with periodicals, were placed a few couches. Il Signore Gambini apparently was a habitué here, for he was able to get me an appointment immediately and, while he ordered us a couple of *camparis*, I walked around the waiting room, dwelling in front of a demoralizing seascape that decorated the wall. A young lady soon called for me, invited me into one of the small rooms and asked me to take off my shoes. *Tutte due*, I said, indicating my shoes. All right. I took off my shoes and my long socks, which I tucked into my shoes and placed with care by the wall, and, while she was getting settled on a stool, I sat down across from her and delicately sunk my heel in between her thighs, in a little snug and malleable nest of the softest terry towel. She carefully grabbed one of my feet, tickling my malleolus bone in doing so, and, handling my foot rather roughly, examined first the sole, then the nails, and finally the toes, one by one, which she spread apart with her finger tips before looking closely at one of the gaps in between, which she considered with profound interest, whistling out of admiration. Bringing her work-kit to her side, she drew out a formidable little tool and, while she busied herself between my toes, I caught site of Il Signore Gambini sitting comfortably on one of the couches in the lounge. With his attaché case open on his knees, he was taking out various documents that he read over quickly, taking a sip of *campari* from time to time. After a little while, as the pedicure was taking some time, he ended up coming over, hands in pockets, to see what was going on; leaning over the young lady's work to demonstrate his concern for my feet, he even went so far in his role as host to display exquisite courtesy in exchanging a few words with her on the nature of my calluses. Corns, he translated for me, lightheartedly, plain-old corns, and he went back to the lounge to get my glass of *campari*. I took a small sip of it while the young lady finished bandaging my toes. Then she went to put her work-kit back on the shelf and, while I was putting my shoes back on, Il Signore Gambini, who just wanted to check something, took his off in the little room, and, sliding off his sock, he lifted up his foot, shifting it sideways to show the young lady, turning her attention towards the big toe's nail which, remarkably contracted indeed, presented the risk of becoming ingrown. They had a long conversation in Italian about this, too technical, to be honest, for me to get involved, but, taking part in looking at the hairy foot demanding our expert opinion, I followed the conversation with a worried look, nodding my head from time to time in sympathy. It was nothing serious, I assure you right away, and, comforted by the young lady, Il Signore Gambini put his sock back on and we left the room carrying our empty glasses with us.

In the street, while we were heading for a small restaurant where Il Signore Gambini had invited me to lunch, I walked with my head lowered, delightfully wiggling my toes inside my shoes; the tickling caused by the bandages was far from unpleasant, and I looked at Il Signore Gambini with heart-felt gratitude (he had little hairs in his nose, I noticed). Reaching the restaurant, we were welcomed by a waiter who gave us some *dottore* before leading us to a back terrace, protected from the looks of outsiders by a wattle fence, with a latticed pergola on which spread a generous vegetation of wild ivy. A ray of light, here and there, glistened on the tablecloths billowed by the wind that gently rustled the leaves. We were brought olives in a saucer and two more *camparis*, and, while Il Signore Gambini spoke to me about the conference that we had attended the day before, opening frequently his attaché case in order to take out some paperwork, he picked at the olives occasionally, which he would then toss in the air and catch in his mouth. There were obviously some silent moments in his speech, interrupting himself each time he tossed one up; but, not losing his train of thought, placing his elbows on the table, he would pick right back up where he left off while discretely spitting out the pit into the palm of his hand. I, too, took an olive from the saucer, just one olive that I had placed on my plate and that I was looking at pensively, working it over with the back of my fork while listening to Il Signore Gambini. To make myself more at home, I had taken my shoes off under the table and was gently rubbing my socked feet together. No longer listening to what Il Signore Gambini was saying, and, focusing all my attention on the olive, which I was continuing, nonchalantly, to wear down on my plate, leaving little lined impressions of my fork on its surface, I could almost physically feel the olive's resistance diminishing. Before too long (at about the same time Il Signore Gambini took an interest in what I was doing and became quiet), the olive seemed ready, and with a swift movement, I stuck my fork into it. Then, looking distractedly at it impaled on my fork, I slowly twirled it before me and, delicately, I pulled it off with my lips.

Before boarding my plane the next morning, I warmly thanked Il Signore Gambini for all that he had done for me in Milan, and, upon arriving in Paris, without losing time, I went to see the young lady at the driver's ed office (don't get up, I said entering, don't get up). I had started reading my newspaper again in front of the projection screen, and the young lady, next to me, with her jacket over her shoulders, had taken out a pile of applications from her drawer and was going through them one by one. At times, continuing to write, she would shiver and, with one hand, barely catch her jacket from slipping off her shoulder. As she was really cold, she got up, a coat covering her shoulders, and, pushing aside a chintz curtain, left to look for another portable heater in a tiny dark storage room, where, in a shower no longer used, next to an azure anorak dangling on a hanger, were stacked several piles of papers. She had asked me to follow her to help her look and, while I pensively flipped through some old registration applications in the darkness, she moved a poorly closed box spilling over with orange parking cones and found a small propane tank for cooking topped with a little radiator with a grilled front. I brought the tank into the room, and, both of us crouching down in front of the radiator, holding the instructions, we tried to figure out how it worked, before realizing that the propane tank was empty. I was more than willing to go to fill up the tank myself, but, as the propane depot could only be reached by car, she suggested that we go there together, explaining to me that it didn't matter at all if we closed the office for an hour or two, she did it quite often in fact, sometimes for no other reason than just to go to the movies. We left the driver's ed office, and, while I was waiting for her on the sidewalk, flipping through my newspaper, she locked up the office and explained to me that, since her Volvo was parked rather far away, we were going to take the driver's ed car, a small orange and white car parked right there, with dual control and a student driver sign on the hood. I put the tank in the trunk and went to sit down in the front seat while she started the car (what a team we made, good God!).

Having left the big avenues of the city, we got on to a sort of access road under construction, where, here and there, between metal barriers displaying various thorny configurations, other driver's ed cars were carrying out cautious maneuvers in reverse. She honked and zigzagged with ease amongst these albatrosses, before stopping next to a man in his forties wearing a buttoned-up parka, smoking on the side of the road and rubbing his cheek with little care or concern. It's one of the instructors, she said. Uh-oh, I said, sounds like trouble. I'm going to talk to him for a second, she said. She got out, then came back to the car right away, leaning over at my window and asking me for the keys to the office that were in her purse. I placed the purse on my knees and began looking through it. Hey, what's this, I said taking out a large envelope. It's nothing, don't worry about it, it's a Pap smear. A little Pap smear, I said, tenderly. But you should send it in, really, you have to send it in. You're sweet, she said. Oh yeah, really, you should send Pap smears in, you know. And it's there inside, I said, dream-like, shaking the envelope next to my ear. Yeah, where else would it be? she said. I didn't know. I put the envelope back in its place, doubtful, the Pap smear couldn't have been a fresh sample, inside such an envelope, in my opinion, and I started looking for the keys again. I found them at the bottom of the purse and handed them to her through the window. Then, while I was waiting in the car and she was conversing on the shoulder with my future instructor (he was wearing some nice canvas boots, I must say), turning away, I took off my shoes, pensive, and, removing a sock which I laid flat on the glove box, I examined my toes for a second, then proceeded to massage my foot with a mixture of firmness and gentleness, grimacing with satisfaction. The young lady opened the door to get back in the car with me, and, a little annoyed by my bare feet (bare feet are always annoying in a car), I explained to her that my foot was asleep and confessed that it appeared to be some kind of rheumatism, apparently due to my bad circulation, I was rather prone to it, to be honest. Yes, rheumatism. Or a little bit of arthritis, wouldn't that be horrible. Well you've seen a doctor right? she asked me. No, no, I said. Because you may have gout, she said. Gout! I screamed, gout on my feet! Sure, she said, gout, and we laughed. We got along rather well, you know, me and her. She put the car into first gear and started it up, as sleepy looking as always, firmly honking at another driver's ed car, and I felt all mournful next to her (maybe it was already love, that flu-like state). Reaching the propane gas depot, which happened to be in a big service station consisting of several buildings and a work garage, at the door of which a mechanic, blowing on his hands, was feeling cold, I caught sight of the plate glass windows of a corner store behind the gasoline pumps and, expecting to find cigarettes there, I got out of the car and told the young lady that I was going to buy some, I hardly had any left. I began walking towards the store and, turning around, asked her if she wanted me to get her something, Mars bar or something nutty, a Milky-Way, what do I know, a Crunch bar. Some chips, she said, and she smiled. A couple that had just walked past me turned around, one looking towards the young lady and the other towards me, and they followed our conversation with interest. You wouldn't rather have something a little better? I said rubbing the tips of my fingers together suggestively, some salted peanuts, a dried fruit mix, some cheese snacks? Sure, sure, she said, whatever you like, and, opening the trunk, she took out the propane tank. All right. I had hardly taken a step forward. Some cheese snacks, good God. I continued walking in my mournful way towards the store and passed through the revolving door at the entrance. There weren't a lot of people there, almost no one in the aisles; an Asian man in a fur-lined jacket was writing a check at the register. I stepped further into the store and walked around, hands in pockets, looking aimlessly at the shelves where, in different sorts of packages, in plastic and in carton, jacks, headlights, and other such stupidities were displayed. Returning to the register, I walked up to the counter and set about choosing an assortment of snacks, which I piled up in my arms as I went along under the suspicious look of the cashier who was on the phone. Then, carefully placing everything down one by one on the counter, I decided after all that I would get some chips, and, walking back down the first aisle, I grabbed a pack off the shelf. How much do I owe you? I asked. The man put his hand over the phone receiver and looked at me inquiringly. For the bag of chips, I said, and, pointing, I also turned his attention to the bill I had put on the counter (I had to tell him everything). Leaving the store, I walked around the building and spotted the bathroom, a flat-roofed, whitewashed pavilion, not too far off in the distance, at the edge of a wasteland where burning tires smouldered. It was a rather dirty place covered in white enamel, where, next to a ragged mop, stretched a row of urinals that stood at an ideal height for someone that would come up to my shoulders. There were also several individual stalls that all had their doors open. I peeked into a number of them before choosing the last one I saw—this was usually the way I went about doing it. I closed the door behind me, bolted it, sat down to piss. I stared blankly at a lizard in the corner of the wall. A faucet was dripping, drop by drop, behind the stall door, a transistor radio could be heard in the distance. Sitting there for a while now, expressionless, perfectly pensive, I was meditating peacefully, pissing being for me rather conducive to thought, I must say. From the second I sit down, really, it takes me no more than ten seconds before I slide into a delightfully blurry and steady world brought forth by my state of mind, and it's tricky to extract myself from this when reclined with my shoulders against the wall, having comfortably taken refuge in my thoughts. I picked up the bag of chips that I had put on the ground and opened it, then looked inside it for a second, skeptical. I grabbed a couple chips and brought them up to my mouth. There was no reason for bringing this entelechy to an end too hastily. Thought, it appeared to me, is a moving stream that is best left alone so that it can expand, unaware of its own flow, and continue to rise naturally, creating innumerable and magnificent branchings that end up mysteriously converging towards a fixed and fleeting point. Let us desire, if it whets our interest, to isolate a thought, a single thought in its passing, and, having considered it from every angle and turned it around in order to better observe it, let us take pleasure in working it over in our minds like modeling clay (why not?); but trying to formulate it is just as disappointing, *in fine*, as the result of a rushed attempt, where the flocculation may seem as miraculous as the precipitated chemical reaction poor and pitiful, a powdery deposit on a microscope cover glass. No, it's better to let thought attend to its serene affairs without any disturbances and, feigning to lose interest in its activities, let oneself be gently rocked by its murmur in order to tend noiselessly towards an understanding of what it is. That was in any case what, at that time, I was aiming to do.

I learned very little from the driving classes that I took some ten years ago. In a driver's ed car, my instructor, a plump, blond, bald man in his fifties who invariably wore a tight, beige cardigan, would pick me up at my house at a specified time. I'd wait for him on the sidewalk and stare at the corner of the street out from where the typical, little vehicle, which was almost completely filled with his large figure, would emerge. He would park the car in front of me and, switching seats with difficulty as his raised pants leg revealed a stealthy calf and a wilted sock, re-adjust his pants and, finally comfortably settled in his new seat, have me start the car while he'd sit looking overwhelmed and gloomy. Then, spending half of the lesson cleaning his glasses with a handkerchief while wearing an annoying angelic smile, and the other half testing the newly acquired transparency of his lenses, he'd lead me through a maze of streets that he knew by heart, making brief commands by gesturing with the frames of his glasses. Methodically, for my part, I'd go up through the gears (I'm not inventing anything here), one foot on the clutch, and the other in a set position, ready at any given moment to impose the weight of my foot on the accelerator. Oppressed and tense during this drill, I'd roll down my window while stopped at a red-light and, looking outside distractedly, I'd tap on the steering wheel to calm my nerves, casually nodding here and there at young female drivers to let them know that everything was going smoothly, that I was having no trouble remaining master of the situation. Don't panic, don't panic. As soon as the light turned green, letting go of the hand brake with an imperceptible shrug of my shoulder, I'd move into first (oh fuck, just to think about it), and, taking my foot off of the clutch, I'd simultaneously press the gas pedal, which would at times move by itself under my foot, driven by a parallel pressure exerted on the double controls by an anonymous foot. My instructor, dozing by my side, would pretend to have no reason to be there and, smiling at me fatalistically, would fall back to sleep as soon as he got comfortable in his seat again. Sometimes, having forgotten that he was there for a while, he'd remind me of his presence by criticizing a minor annoying detail, such as the incorrect positioning of the steering wheel; his torso wouldn't move, but his hand would mechanically make a slight gesture to indicate that I had to skirt as much as possible an upcoming obstacle, which was precisely what I was in the process of doing with the utmost concern. As, little by little, the exams were coming up, I could no longer neglect preparing myself for the written tests (I had indeed started taking driving lessons before taking the class—to get ahead, in a way, you know me). Thus, at home, I'd leaf through an illustrated driver's manual in an offhand way, a book adorned with a selection of colored photos displaying a televisual aesthetic based on a police comedy, where the invisible guilty party, always the same, presented under the unsettling, subjective point of view of various framings, would be at the wheel in a number of different towns and configurations, in the sun or in the rain, sometimes on deserted country roads, where some cyclist wearing a cagoule and a red helmet, bike rack flanked with panniers, would appear to be the designated victim. The psychology of the assassin—me, in this case—laid bare all throughout the text, was presented in the form of maxims stated in the first person, such as *I do not move my vehicle, not even a meter, if the windshield is not clear or transparent.* With me, there was no risk, I had trust in myself, and, lying on my bed, I'd continue to flip through the book at random; I'd pick it up a few times every day and I ended up regarding it as a leisure read, which, during breakfast for example, allowed me to solve futile brain-teasers composed of stylish cars and cross-roads, routes, and signs, all illustrated with cute little diagrams on a green background made with the most hideous graphics. Familiarizing myself rather quickly with the questions known to be tricky, I took note of the most complex situations that were likely to show up on the test and, as I have always been a quick thinker—I mean, let it be understood, no one can be expected to do the impossible—hardly had I perceived the arrangement of the cars, that I then established which had the right of way. Wouldn't even take me ten seconds. 1. Red. 2. Blue. That's an example. 1. Yellow. 2. Blue. 3. Green. You see? At night sometimes I would head over to the driver's ed office, where, during classes, I could practice my skills in real test-like conditions. In the darkened room, sitting next to a pale and melancholic girl, I'd watch the transparencies pass one after the other on the overhead projector and write down the answers to the test questions as if in a dream. My neighbor, lost and charming, who seemed to be getting pissed off by this exercise, she looked rather British, would peek discretely at my notebook and copy with an utter lack of concern my answers onto her paper. She cheated without a guilty conscience, oh yeah she did, with an indifference that made her proud, and never appeared to be surprised by her brilliant and ever-correct responses, which earned her enthusiastic and vaguely paternalistic encouragements from the teacher, a supportive guy in a leather jacket and tie who spoke in flourished terms and sported a goatee. He took a disliking to me rather quickly, this man, but he never turned his attention away from my neighbor, pulling her aside to ask her questions and give her personal advice with his small hand on her shoulder, granting us the repugnant sight of his hairy finger slipping in and out of his signet ring while he massaged her adorable shoulder. During class, he'd stand up on stage and meticulously set up his small magnetic toy cars on the worktable, explaining in detail after extraneous detail the need of yielding, moving his index finger from one car to another. At times, to spice up his explanations, he'd indulge in the delight of telling a little joke, which he'd deliver while mischievously stroking his goatee, and, witnessing the class's reaction and boiling over with self-satisfaction, he'd smile gratefully in response to our chuckles. For a reason that must have eluded him, he could never get a single rejoinder out of us seven or eight students spread out throughout the classroom; my neighbor would look at the wall, for example, or up at the ceiling, and the young man with a scarf sitting in front of me would continue to draw fighter planes in his notebook. At the end of class, while our little group dispersed in front of the school, the class instructor would zip up his jacket, stopping before reaching the neck so as to leave a flattering glimpse of his straightened tie, and, taking in a deep breath of the night air, playing it cool, he'd offer to give my neighbor a ride home. Feeling a little too lazy to walk home, for my part, I'd sometimes generously offer to accompany them (we all lived close to the school, it seemed, except of course for the instructor). He had an old car fixed up like new that smelled like air-freshener, with seat covers insanely well taken care of, nonadjustable neck rests and a noctilucent luck charm that swung back and forth in front of the windshield. As he gave us a tour of the area (it really was just next door, I'm telling you), he leaned forward to turn on his music system and, back speakers going off on each side of the car, an affectionate serenade began in the darkness, which, in my absence, would have probably allowed him to take advantage of the romantic mood of the musical setting, letting himself go with weary gestures, one hand on the wheel, confident in his plans and ambitions, his hopes and fears. Well, I was the one in the front—yes, yes, I prefer to take the front seat, I told him—and, during the ride, while he let us know in an offhand way that his multifunctional music system was digital, eyeing his rearview mirror to see the effect that this comment would produce on my neighbor, he gave us a demonstration to show us the capabilities of this jewel, choosing the radio for example (simple example) modulating the frequencies with a feeling of serene and detached control, while, lighting up in red on the luminescent display screen, lineaments of broken crystal liquid sprung forth frantically at the touch of his finger. The first time that he gave me a ride home, I remember, I was rather surprised to see my neighbor get out at my stop, and, lingering with her on the sidewalk while the instructor's car drove off in the distance, we talked for a little while in front of my door. She was leaning against it, suggestively, her hand in her hair, seemingly not ready to go her separate way. I ignored what she was going after and, as the silence was becoming heavy, we strove to find, from time to time, questions to ask each other. Eyes lowered, I deeply thought over each response, toying pensively with her coat-strap. Then, with both of us finally saying goodbye to go back to our own places, I realized that we live in the same building. Driving lessons, in the meantime, followed their course. I had to have been at my seventh or eighth lesson, and my instructor continued to pick me up at my house at an early hour; we still followed the same itinerary, a few variations now and then, which consisted of a journey not too different from that of the knight in Breyer's Gambit, that is to say, a short drive around the neighborhood, very slow and almost indecisive, executed with indifference to the other pieces of the board (an interesting variant that this Breyer, all in apparent retreat and circumspect evasions, as if nothing was going on, would lay the foundation of a solid position). I don't know at all if I was progressing in my mastery of driving, but, after a few classes, beginning to get tired of the endless monotony of the practice route, I ended up suggesting to my instructor that we spend fifteen minutes of the lesson in a café. This soon became a regular part of our schedule—taking a fifteen-minute break—and, it seemed to me, it worked out well for the both of us. We didn't have a preferred café, no, we just chose one at random, although our choice often happened to be the same brasserie on the corner of the street that we usually took on our way back. It was a lively place, refurbished quite some time ago, with large wall mirrors and a packfong counter, glossy and bright, backed by shelves lined with all sorts of cocktail bottles topped with measuring caps, standing either upright or attached upside-down to the wall. We'd come in through glass double doors that opened up directly to the bar, and then immediately grab a seat at a nearby table. I'd sit on the banquette, and he, Fulmar, would take the chair (because, if the class instructor's name was Puffin, Jean-Claude Puffin, my driving instructor's name was Fulmar; and in class everyone was saying that they lunched together everyday, Puffin and Fulmar, in a restaurant where they had their regular table). Sitting there, we'd usually have an espresso making the wise decision to resist throwing in a calvados along with it. We, my instructor and I, obviously didn't have a relationship like the one he shared with Puffin, and, both of us remaining rather reserved, we'd stir our espressos in silence, my instructor turning around at times to keep an eye on the driver's ed car which was parked in front of the building and which, from our table, well-chosen, we could leisurely contemplate. From time to time we would take a sip, then place the espresso cup back down on the saucer. We'd look all around casually, tapping the table with a cardboard beer coaster. At times, a few words were spoken, concerning a certain type of beer, for example, provoked by the fact that its logo was displayed on the front of the coaster. Tuborg, he would remark, nodding his head lost in thought. Yep, I'd say,

Tuborg. I'd then find it appropriate to bring up other beers that were served on tap at the brasserie. He'd sit unresponsive, putting his coaster on its side and balancing it with his finger. A Danish beer, I'd say, Tuborg's Danish. He knew that, and would nod his head to express that he knew it. I knew that, he'd say. Yep, a Danish beer, and, sighing, he'd take a small sip of his espresso. We'd each pay for our own drink, because I had treated him the first time, and, since then, he insisted in an almost friendly way that we split the bill. I could have considered him perfect, this man, if, one day while he was dozing next to me in the car, his hands folded over his stomach, fiddling mischievously with his glasses, the distressing idea hadn't come to him to make me parallel park. The morning in question, sporting a new pull-over, black and close-fitting, in favor of his usual sweater-vest, tag still hanging from his collar and having changed his usual morning greeting to a "Come with me, young man" greeting, he directed me towards a supermarket parking lot that he pointed to with his glasses and, having me go around several annexed buildings, led me to a back lot where workers unloaded refrigerated delivery trucks in front of metal warehouses. He got out of the car while readjusting his pants and went around back to take a pile of stacked cones out of the trunk, which he casually placed alongside the sidewalk, his tag flapping behind him (I eyed it thoughtfully, forearms resting on the wheel), before coming back to lean through the window, one hand on the hood, inviting me (here's the rundown, he said) to park the car in the space he'd just created. He then went to stand back a little further and, lighting up a small cigar, he glanced over at the warehouses. One of the workers soon approached him and, holding packaged ham, distractedly watched me maneuver around. I watched them through the rearview mirror as they exchanged a few words; my instructor had taken out a yellow plastic sack from his pocket, which he unfolded slowly, methodically, and, suddenly—everything happened so quickly—he slipped the worker some money who, for his part, gave him the ham in exchange. He immediately stashed it in the plastic sack and, the ham now hidden, smoothing out the folds in the plastic, he looked around, feigning to be calm, making sure that no one had caught sight of their deal. I'd finished parking the car and my instructor, who must have figured that we'd done enough parallel parking for the day, began picking up the cones around the car, before putting everything in the trunk, the cones tossed with little concern, the ham with precautionary care, tucked with love behind the spare tire. He sat down next to me in the front and, while we were leaving the parking lot, he looked closely at his watch and, as if reluctantly, had me take the route back. Personally, I would have easily driven to my house (to drop myself off), but, at the end of class, he preferred that I drive to the school where another student would be waiting for him. This same day, getting out of the car with me, he let my young successor know that he'd be back in a couple of minutes and, opening the trunk to get the ham, he entered the school with his package under his arm. I followed him in so that I could set up another driving session, and, as the secretary was busy (a fine-looking lady, this secretary, with a teenage-girlish pair of glasses sparkling with colored frames), I sat waiting until she finished writing a letter, while my instructor tidied up his locker, in which there was a thermos, as well as chamois skin and a few magazines. He got up on his tip toes and made room for his package, while on his back, true to form, his tag fluttered. I lit up a cigarette, and watched his tag absentmindedly, tapping my thigh with my hand. The secretary assured me that she'd be with me in a second and, finishing her letter written in turquoise ink (turquoise, good God, turquoise ink), let me know while writing that it seemed to her that my application was still missing some documents. She lifted up her head and smiled, shaking her finger at me shamefully. What kind of documents, my darling? She reread her letter, content, and, putting it into an envelope, wet the edges with two quick, moist slides of the tongue. Well let's see, she said, and, opening a drawer, she looked through the filed applications before selecting mine, which she laid open on the table. My instructor, who had safely stowed away his ham, had poured himself a small cup of café au lait and was standing next to us; he was facing the door, holding his thermos, and looking outside. Your back, Fulmar, the secretary pointed out to him. A tag, dear, your tag is still on, and, smiling at me and raising her eyes to the sky, she continued to go through my application. Actually, I wasn't missing anything important, apart maybe from my medical paperwork, and I promised her I'd bring it the day after tomorrow, a day that I took advantage of to set up a driving session. We continued to chat about this and that, trying to set straight the problems that had not yet been dealt with (my passport photos, for example, which I admitted I also still needed to bring).

The bathroom at the service station was nice and quiet, and, beyond my stall door, I could hear running water, off in the distance, the crackling of a transistor radio. I could see that the door, across from me, gray and dirty, was closed; a little bolt, resting on a support structure attached to the door, loose and missing three out of four screws, kept it closed. Up till now no one had come to disturb me, and I lingered there peacefully, thinking about this chess problem that Breyer had composed in which all the opponent's pieces were vulnerable and the board controlled, which was due to the fact that during the last fifty moves not a single pawn had been moved nor a single piece captured. This problem (personally, I didn't see the problem), which had been delightfully occupying my mind for a while now, seemed to me to represent a modus vivendi of the utmost refinement. Even in his official matches, Breyer displayed the same courtesy, wisely guarding all his pieces behind closed lines and preparing long-range plans of attack which, firstly, simply consisted of increasing with infinite, miniscule refinements the degree of his pieces' dynamic potential (and, secondly, massacring). Although Breyer's ideas had been validated by the amount of success obtained when tested in real life, they provoked public skepticism, even suspicion at times, as they gave rise to paradoxical lines of play, in which the design followed was never clearly defined and in which the pieces, following a twisted logic of conserving endlessly-accumulating energy, systematically failed to fulfill their duty of seeking out freedom to move. And, while I continued to linger in the stall tranquilly following the course of my thoughts, I vaguely felt that the reality with which I was grappling was beginning little by little to show some signs of fatigue; it was beginning to soften and slacken, oh yes it was, and I had no doubt that my repeated assaults, in their tranquil persistence, would end up exhausting reality little by little, as one wears out an olive with a fork, if you will, by pushing down on it lightly from time to time, and that when, weary, reality finally offers no more resistance, I knew that nothing could then stop my impetus, a furious surge that had always been in me, strengthened by everything I had accomplished. But, for the time being, I had all the time in the world: in the battle between oneself and reality, don't try to be courageous. I finally got out of the stall, still just as pensive (I would make quite some thinker, indeed), and, closing the door behind me, I walked towards the row of mirrors above the sinks. I put my hand in front of my mouth, striking a pose that seemed rather flattering to me, and skeptically pondered this impenetrable look, which I had believed fit me well (a hard look, an implacable expression), when, behind me, a man came in who, having briefly glanced at me, told me that there was a young lady outside who had been looking for someone for a while now. I figure it's you, he told me. Yeah, maybe. I left him to his doubts, and, leaving the bathroom, I headed back over towards the service station, hands in coat pockets (it was a Stanley Blacker—you know, not that bad of a coat). Back in the open lot, I looked all around me, squinting to find the young lady. There was not a lot going on at this service station, nothing really at all. A lady walked across the parking lot to join her husband who was waiting for her at the wheel of his Volkswagen. As for the young lady, well, I didn't see a single trace of her, but our little orange and white car, however, proudly flaunting its student-driver sign, was still there, poorly parked right where we had left it. Finally, I ended up walking around the store in the other direction and, skirting the conjoining buildings, found myself in a new parking lot, much smaller, where the young lady was waiting with the propane tank. I apologized for taking so long and got ready to head back to the car with her when, lifting up the tank, I realized that it was still empty. She watched me set it back down on the ground, without saying anything, and pointed to a guy off in the distance, standing next to a large cage in which, behind metal bars, were placed rows of gas bottles. She explained to me that this man, who was spying on us as we talked, had not only refused to serve her, but had practically insulted her. I looked down, fatalist, and pensively kicked up dust from the ground. Ok, I said, I'll see what I can do. I went to go talk to him (this guy was going to hear from me, damn it). What is this I hear, I asked, it appears that you were rude with my wife. Ah, no, not at all, I assure you, he hastened to protest, and he quickly let me know that he had simply explained to her that he only has *thermo gaz*, and that, because of this, he wasn't able to fill up her tank, which was *prima gaz*, because even if he had accepted to fill it up, he was saying, the *thermo gaz* distributors would definitely not exchange it, he had already been through this once with *naph ta gaz*. You mean *prima gaz*, I said, as a small clarification, understanding that it was easy for him to mix them up. No, no, he said, it was *naph ta gaz*. All right. But tell me, I said taking my hand out of my pocket, if you have already been through this misunderstanding once with *naph ta gaz*, it means that you have indeed refilled tanks which were not *thermo gaz*. He had to have seen my point. And you refuse to do the same favor for my wife! I said. I was on a roll. He nodded his head, perturbed, ready to admit that he'd been defeated by the byzantinian finesse of my reasoning and, on the verge of letting himself be convinced, he assured me that if it were up to him, well of course he would have refilled it, but with the *thermo gaz* distributors it wasn't even worth discussing, and that, if he accepted to refill it for us, it would end up costing him his job, a prospect he could not come to terms with, even if it would, as it appeared to me, be best for everyone. We argued a little bit more and, facing the persistence of his overwhelmed casuistry, I forgot about it and asked him where we could find some *prima gaz*. I'm not really sure, he said, you can always look at Mammouth. You think they'll have it? I asked, skeptical. Uh, it's possible, he said, it's possible. I don't see any other options, he added, and, that being all he could unfortunately do for me, he explained how to get there. I went to tell the young lady the good news, that, there you have it, it was all taken care of, we'll probably find some at Mammouth. At Mammouth, good God. I picked up the tank, and we went back to the open lot. We walked side by side, I was carrying the tank. By the way, I said, I told him you were my wife. Good thinking, she said. Speaking of which, what's your name? Pascale, her name was Pascale Polougaïevski. What a day. In the car, while we slowly pulled out of the parking lot, I explained to her, head cushioned against the neck rest, that my lower spine was sore, always the same back problem, and, as she was kind enough to take an interest in my problem, and rather intelligently I must say, I took pleasure in relating to her the ins and outs of the whole ordeal. That's why, I said, for the propane tank, I'll carry it as long as it's empty, but when it's full . . . She looked at me. Well, it wouldn't be too wise, I said. I looked outside absently; we were driving through a wasteland; off in the distance I could make out uniform housing developments.

Back at the driver's ed office, in the middle of the afternoon (we still hadn't filled up the propane tank, no, it wasn't even worth talking about), the young lady noticed her father who was scraping something off of the sole of his shoe in front of the office, shopping basket in hand, wearing an astrakhan hat with earflaps. M. Polougaïevski, to whom I was introduced on the sidewalk, was a rather plump man with Baltic cheek bones and a strong Russian accent, who, after listening to his daughter explain our situation while he swung his shopping basket back and forth, suggested that we all immediately go to Créteil to get another propane tank (all right kids, let's hit the road, he said, and he had us get into his car, an old rundown Triumph). The shopping center was still not in sight and, while M. Polougaïevski, leaning over the wheel of his Triumph, flew along the beltway at top speed, I dozed in the backseat thinking about the fact that the reality with which I was grappling, far from showing the slightest signs of wearing out, seemed to have little by little hardened all around me and, finding myself henceforth incapable of extracting myself from this stone reality that was enclosing me on all sides, I presently viewed my impetus as a surge of releasing forces forever imprisoned in stone. I could have easily had a little muscadet wine while waiting, you know, and, remaining still in the backseat, impassive and on the verge of sleep, I privately took pleasure in this feeling of letting things follow their course, not planning on even lifting a finger in this affair. Having reached the shopping center, M. Polougaïevski went to ask if they had propane tanks, and, letting him talk to a person at the information desk, a gloomy lady who watched him make emphatic, extravagant gestures at the counter while he explained what he wanted with his flamboyant and variegated accent, I snuck off and wandered around the store, ending up indulging in a guilty pleasure: I let myself be tempted by a package of disposable razors and shaving cream. While waiting in line to pay, I caught sight of M. Polougaïevski who was busy reading flyers next to the entrance, and who, unaware that I was watching him, was in the process of jotting down a number in his address book. I quickly put the razors in a plastic bag and walked over towards him. He checked one last time to make sure he wrote down the number correctly and, closing his address book with a look of mysterious satisfaction, he told me that we had to go back to the car, that the gas depot was at the service station at the entrance of the parking lot. After having refilled the tank, we placed it in the trunk of the car and went to take shelter from the rain while waiting for his daughter, who had gone to pick up a few groceries at a neighboring store, to get back. I got in the front seat, M. Polougaïevski sat behind the wheel, and from the crack of our open door we watched the raindrops dot the surface of a puddle of water. The radio was playing a sad, sweet song and both of us, sitting quietly, began to bob our heads back and forth thoughtfully as if we were sharing this moment. Then, as his daughter had still not come out of the store and as the crooning had become harsh and loud, he turned toward me to see if I was paying attention. What the hell could she be doing? he said, and, getting out of the car, hands deep in his pockets, he stared impatiently at the store entrance. Pascale came out unexpectedly several minutes later, with a huge box full of groceries. I let her take the front seat and got in the back, placing the box next to me while her father started the car, well *tried* to start the car (it's not starting, he said). We finally got out of the Triumph, his daughter and I—

what a family—and began pushing the car in the rain, following the contradictory instructions that her father was giving us with his head out the window. As this got us nowhere, trying something else, Pascale took the wheel and, after having reached a slight declivity, her father and I began pushing from either side while the car gave some promising jolts that made us push even harder and yell up to Pascale to step on it, before ending by us giving up, feet and socks soaked, and walking up towards Pascale. So? her father said leaning over her window (it's dead, she said).

In a much more relaxed way, combining our efforts but without overdoing it, we pushed the car to the service station. I was pushing with both of my hands placed on the back of the car while M. Polougaïevski, stooped over with fatigue and breathing heavily, walked alongside me, sheltering himself from the rain with my newspaper while explaining to me that it was probably due to the humidity, good grief (yeah, yeah I'm sure, I said, watching the rain soak my newspaper). When the service station was in sight, we could see the man who sold us the propane tank, a cryptic kind of guy, thin with greasy hair, who was suspiciously sniffing his fingers, looking at us with an air of complete mistrust as we approached. We stopped the car in front of the gas pumps and, explaining to him what had happened, asked him if he could take a look at the engine. He could not, nope, it wasn't his responsibility, the mechanic would be there soon, and he invited us to wait in his office. He sat down at his desk next to his racing bike, an old mountain bike with threadbare bungee cords, and we waited across from him, M. Polougaïevski and I seated in folding chairs, and Pascale standing in front of the window, looking out pensively. A couple posters hung on the wall, as well as a calendar given away by a liquor company. We weren't talking at all, not a single one of us, and the man kept to his own business. He took out a Mikado game from his drawer and, maneuvering the sticks quite well between his hands, placed them gently on his desk before beginning to pick them back up one by one. From time to time, we exchanged a few words with him, formulating a few hypotheses regarding the possible causes of our car trouble. He would nod his head thoughtfully in agreement at times and, skeptically examining the entangled jumble of sticks, admit that, yeah sure, it could be the ignition. Or the spark plugs, could be that too, and, after a moment of hesitation during which he seemed to be thinking hard about the question, he snatched with a swift and precise movement of the hand one of the little sticks between his fingers (I got you didn't I, you little bastard, he said as he delicately placed it next to him). M. Polougaïevski, frowning, watched him play while, for my part, I had taken the packet of razors out of my pocket and, looking at the sink, I wondered if the man would find it improper of me to shave while waiting, I hadn't had time in the morning. He didn't seem too upset, no, when I asked permission, but, putting his Mikado game on hold for a second, he turned around to move his bike out of the way and, while studying with absorption the position of the sticks, he moved forward a little bit to let me pass. I went around his desk, thanked him, and, placing my razors and shaving cream alongside the sink, began to unbutton my shirt, then rubbed my chest absent-mindedly while looking around. I had hung on a nail a pocket mirror that Pascale had given me and, feeling that I was lacking sufficient space to shave, I had to stand on my toes next to the man playing Mikado, twisting around when necessary in order to rinse my razor under the faucet, glancing distractedly at the position of the motley-colored sticks spread out on the desk. In the upper corner of my mirror I could see Pascale, who was looking out the window while her father, in the folding chair, had moved close to the desk in order to give his unwelcomed advice on the game, angrily insisting with a pointed finger that the man go after this stick rather than another. The man, for his part, whom I could see in the lower part of the mirror while I continued to shave my cheeks, seemed quite reticent and troubled about which stick to go after. I picked up my things when I had finished and, putting my shirt back on (I didn't feel comfortable leaving it off in this office), I went outside to get some fresh air, nonchalantly rubbing off the shaving cream that remained hanging on my earlobes. M. Polougaïevski came to join me after a little while, and we lingered around the car waiting for the mechanic to show up. He seemed perturbed, I thought, M. Polougaïevski, and, telling me that we'd probably have to leave the car here to be repaired, he suggested we take a taxi at once. Can we use your phone? he asked the man after going back into the office. The man put his finger in front of his lips, solemnly, to silence him, and, studying attentively the layout of the sticks, he approached one with the utmost care, and lifted it like a lever, pressing ever so lightly on the far end. Then, setting it down next to him, he slid the phone over to the other end of his desk for M. Polougaïevski.

Ending up abandoning the idea of trying to find a taxi (sorry, none available), M. Polougaïevski took care of various formalities for getting the Triumph fixed and gave money for the phone calls made in vain for a taxi, and, after giving him the car keys, he asked the man if we could take the propane tank with us because we had already been through a lot to get it. The man, who looked at him while pensively tapping the palm of his hand with a Mikado stick, preferred that we leave it in the trunk of the car and, casually accompanying us outside, he indicated with the slender point of his stick where we'd need to go to catch the metro. Then, returning to his office, he stopped at the threshold and watched us go off in the rain, M. Polougaïevski carrying the box of groceries, me my package of razors and Pascale the car radio her father had preferred to remove from the car. Arriving at the shopping center, we opened the glass double doors at the entrance and, welcomed by a gust of dry heat coming up from a floor vent, we walked down the main strip of the mall. We went along amongst the bustling crowd and, here and there, in front of the opened-door shops, were revolving stands offering various unlabeled designer merchandise. A garden shop had some dried shrubs on display and, continuing to wander around the mall and passing by shops of all sorts, we walked by a beauty salon where ladies who sensed they were being watched tried to look sophisticated while seated under their perm machines, bonjour Mesdames. Leaving the shopping center, momentarily confused about which way to go, we went down a small paved street in the newer area of this suburb, with a row of stylized streetlights placed at regular intervals like derisory and apocryphal accessories. Likewise, the entire neighborhood, with its impersonal and cold architecture, seemed to be a vast model in which we, like pieces fit to scale, leisurely moved about between two rows of buildings. Glass and metal constructions towered at the horizon while, here and there, we'd walk alongside an isolated building that rose up endlessly in the sky, all the windows darkened with blue-tinted panes. Further along, while we were apparently going off in the wrong direction, walking down a little sloping street that continued on interminably, we came upon an immense artificial lake clouded over on the horizon by the grayness of an industrial zone, with giant cranes and factory chimneys emitting long columns of black smoke into the sky. Bordering the lake, fixed up as a place of leisure and relaxation, the names of streets and promenades evoked the south of France and, among this arid and concrete space, stood a deserted restaurant with a terrace in a state of neglect, where closed parasols were getting soaked by the rain. Wavelets from the lake, weary and sluggish, tossed up gently into the mud, forming a sort of gray-colored beach which stretched into a wasteland where there was a wooden hut, tottering like a palafitte, with abandoned, nail-studded boards in front of the door and a broken wishbone lying on the ground, buried in the grass softened and wet from the rain. A few wind-surfing boards in a better state were stored further along the beach, and, on the placid water of the lake, amidst the rain's fog and factory smoke swept along by a light and regular drizzle, some windsurfers in wet suits seemed to be motionless in the absence of wind, straight and still on their stationary boards, trying to gain speed by jerking the sail towards themselves in regular tugs and finally ending up moving slowing through the foggy stretch of water, under the shadow of a giant metal railroad bridge suspended over the lake. We went down to the bank and walked along the lake in the rain, feet sinking in the soggy and muddy sand of the shore. A helicopter flew at a low altitude above us, and I walked looking up, thinking that we must have made an interesting sight to see, marching forward on this beach in a single file, M. Polougaïevski leading the pack with the box of groceries, me following right behind, indifferent and aloof with my coat collar raised, and Pascale still further off, nonchalantly dragging a dead tree branch that she had picked up along the way. In actual fact, M. Polougaïevski was simply looking for someone who could give us directions, and, walking up to the shore, he approached an old, rather thin man who, standing in water up to his waist, was getting ready to go out on his windsurfing board, wearing a short-sleeved, black, tight-fitting wet suit and a ridiculous lifejacket fastened to his exceptionally frail body by way of a network of straps. Having taken a good look at him, M. Polougaïevski walked up to the edge of the water with his box of groceries and asked him from a distance if he knew where the metro station was. The man had apparently not quite understood the question, and, coming back towards us with his hands on the board like a big-time surfer, had us repeat it, before indicating with his agile arm that we'd have to go back up the little street and take a left, which would lead us to the shopping center. It's not even five minutes away, he added, and, carefully getting on his board, one knee first, then the other, he stood straight up before slowly pulling the sail (and fell down hard while we walked off in the distance—in fact, he wasn't that great of a surfer).

Reaching the metro station, we lingered a bit in the ticket office, dark and silent, where a few boy scouts were fooling around. M. Polougaïevski had placed the box of groceries at the foot of a map on the wall to look over the route and, having studied it for quite some time, rubbed his eyes in frustration and concluded, defeated, that he had to change lines at Reuilly-Diderot, and us at Daumesnil, unless we went way out of the way to La Motte-Piquet. I didn't have any preference personally, and Pascale, who had taken out a pack of chips from the grocery box and was snacking, the car radio between her knees, watching dreamily the young scouts in the ticket office, didn't care either apparently. All right kids, let's get going, her father said, picking up the box of groceries, and he led us down the stairs on to the lower level. We walked along the platform while waiting for the metro, and ended up going to sit down on a bench. When the metro arrived, we sat down in a deserted car, which remained empty for a few more stations, not really filling up until we reached the veterinarian school. M. Polougaïevski and his daughter were seated side by side on foldaway seats and I was standing up across from them, reading my paper, leaning up against the pole. From time to time, I looked up and glanced at the names of stations at which we stopped. Reaching Daumesnil, M. Polougaïevski helped us with the box of groceries and I bade him farewell, leaning forward with deference to warmly shake his hand through the open door. Then the doors slammed shut, and we stayed for a second on the platform watching the metro go off into the distance while M. Polougaïevski, standing straight up behind the window of the door, waved with noble sweeps of the arm before giving us little goodbyes with the hand (he's nice, huh? Pascale said).

The following night, Pascale and I were eating alone at an Indian restaurant. I'd found the address by chance in a tourist brochure that I'd picked up when we went down to the hotel lobby, and, back in the room—a rather large room with a view of a park—seated next to the nightstand, I had called to reserve a table, the brochure on my lap and a pen in hand (can you turn down the TV please? Thanks). There wasn't an open table before ten o'clock, which maybe seemed a little late to me, but I made the reservation anyway, thinking that we could always cancel it if we changed our minds. We had gotten to London that same afternoon and, rather fatigued from the trip, we'd looked for a hotel and had gone to bed right away. From our bed, which was next to a window draped with charming, little white curtains, we could see the top of some trees, a patch of sky. We weren't that bad off there, not at all; we had turned on the TV and watched indifferently the afternoon shows, which consisted of a pool tournament accompanied by solemn commentary whispered with an obsolete seriousness. One of the players was a redhead who wore a clear-blue shirt, sleeves rolled up; the other, older, more graceful, looked pained and took more time, maybe, before finally deciding to attempt a difficult, three-cushion shot. The commentator appeared at times as well, sitting in the second row amongst the crowd, a headset on and various papers in his hand, and who, each time that he was aware of being on camera, raised his head, right hand keeping his headset in place. We would smile at each other, Pascale and I, from time to time, and, leaning on my shoulder, she continued, yawning, to watch TV. We finally got dressed to go out, and, as I was ready sooner, I sat on the edge of the bed waiting for her, looking at the hotel menu, which consisted of a whole list of drinks and offered, for the morning, the choice of a continental or a British breakfast (with sausage, mmm, I love sausage). Then, putting the menu down, I checked to make sure that I had money and the address of the restaurant, and we left; our room opened out onto a vestibule with a thick, red carpet, in the center of which stood a decorative edicule, adorned with green plants and imitation, meringue-like colonnades, sweet and affected. We walked around this immaculate thing (I turned around to look at it, dream-like, a hand behind my neck), and, going through the glass door, we went to wait for the elevator. While we were going down in the elevator, I pulled back a loose strand of hair from her eyes. She looked at me. I placed my hand on her shoulder, stroking her cheek tenderly (I have a bit of a headache, I said).

When we left the hotel, our attention was drawn to a crowd gathering not far from us; traffic was completely blocked off and police were coming and going in front of the barricade, some holding dogs by the leash, some with walkie-talkies in their hands. Various fire trucks were parked in the middle of the road, as well as police cars, whose revolving lights flashed slowly in the night. There was also a TV crew setting up their equipment behind the park gates, and a lot of curious spectators all around, both groups waiting for the imminent landing of a hot air balloon in Kensington Gardens. Oh, so that's what it is, she said (yes, I said, that's got to be it). But, actually, I had no idea. It was simply one out of many possible explanations. A hot air balloon with the yellow Shell logo, for example. Or Total's design, I don't know their logo. Some sort of gas company, essentially. But to know something *essentially*, can we really determine the quiddity from a logo? I wasn't so sure. We joined the small group to find out more, and, staying there for a bit trying in vain to understand what was going on, we ended up turning around and heading back in the direction of the restaurant. She was a little cold, my Pascale Polougaïevski, and, stopping at a crosswalk, I took her in my arms to warm her up while, head against my chest and moving her feet in place to get her blood going, she continued to yawn. I also yawned, as you can imagine, yawning being contagious, and we began shaking together on the sidewalk, held tightly in each other's arms, freezing and yawning. I squeezed her against my chest as hard as I could and, having enclosed her in my coat with me, we began jumping up and down together to stay warm, irresistibly going up into the air, locked together silently. When the light changed, she crossed the street running and I ran too, well almost, in order to catch up to her, which shows what kind of mood I was in. We arrived at the restaurant all out of breath and, having found where it was and having looked over the menu, we slowly walked away, our reservation not being until ten. We still had around an hour to kill and, not knowing what to do in the meantime, we wandered around that area, went into a pub, where, having worked my way up to the bar, passing by heavy drinkers with some difficulty, I ordered two beers (yes two, my Lord, I said in my broken English, and I made a V with my fingers to make sure that it was clear), and, carefully picking up the glasses, I slipped between two young bearded men and headed towards a back corner of the bar where we sat on a bench against the wall, next to a slot machine. Before leaving the bar, I couldn't resist putting a few coins in the slot machine, trying my luck, a match in my mouth, pensively lowering the lever. The interior cylinder would spin around and come to a dead stop, showing an odd assortment of fruit, from which two eternal mauve prunes, ambivalent and testicle-shaped, recurrently appeared before me as an image of my personal fate. Pascale had joined me and was watching me play, hand on my shoulder, languid and not too interested. She wanted to try too, and, placing herself in front of the machine, yawning, she lowered the lever forcefully like a truck driver, my God, which caused several people to look at us. She took an interest in the game rather quickly, and, admitting that there was no need to slam the lever down, she lowered it softly, and even won some coins in doing so. Around nine thirty, we began our way to the restaurant. The sky, which I looked up at from time to time, cloudy and moonless, moved with the wind in a procession of dark clouds, drifting silently towards other skies. A neon sign shined in front of the restaurant and we reached the dining area by way of a back terrace, fenced-in, which looked out on the street. On the entrance steps, lit up by a subdued light, stood an Indian man, apparently the host, whom I waved to at a distance, all while fearing that we were a little too early. No not at all, not at all, and, lowering his welcoming face bathed in red light, he let me know regretfully that there were no more tables for two remaining. Full, he said. Full, I said. Full, he said. Well, I said, and, turning back around, I gave Pascale the bad news. But we made a reservation, she said. Yeah, that's what kills me, I said. But you have to insist, she said, and, walking past me, she went up to the host to discuss the matter with him. He was very amicable with her and, going to take another look at the dining area, he came immediately back to the entrance steps and invited us to follow him. It was apparently a rather large restaurant, because, after having led us through a private dining area, we walked into a bright bar decorated in a colonial style, with varnished wooden floors, an old record player against the wall surrounded by plants, rattan couches and a giant ceiling fan that spun with an inexorable slowness. He handed us over to a waiter (overly effusive, in my opinion) who, performing a *rond de jambe*, invited us to sit down. Would you care to try the house drink? he asked. I beg your pardon? I said while taking my seat. He didn't insist on asking again but confiscated our small plate of peanuts from the table. Fifteen minutes passed and, from time to time, he would walk by acting as if he didn't see us. As other people came in sporadically, he would take them into the room, fawning over them, leading them or pushing them forward encouragingly, and, when he came back to the bar after having seated them, reflective, hand covering his mouth, he'd turn towards us to assure us with a conniving and tacit nod that our table would be ready in no time. But I wasn't in any hurry to be seated, for my part. No. Maybe even, looking at the way Pascale was sitting across from me, her head slightly tilted to one side and her bangs falling over her forehead, leaning back and looking at me with bright weary eyes, her cheek now almost touching her shoulder and her beige coat unbuttoned, its belt hanging down to the ground, maybe even in seeing her like this, her outstretched legs and her little feet hidden in big shoes which exposed a bit of white sock at ankle level, maybe I was savoring more the slowness of this moment and the reassuring repose that this delay offered, thinking there was no longer any doubt whatsoever that, for the first time, we were going to eat together, me and her.

Back in Paris, very early on Monday morning, we went to go pick up little Pierre from Pascale's father's house (are you sure that I need to go along? I asked on the landing). M. Polougaïevski greeted us in his bathrobe, hair disheveled, and, calling out to little Pierre who was in the process of getting ready, he looked at his watch in the darkness of the entryway. Did you drive? he asked me. Excuse me? I said. Because little Pierre's school starts at eight o'clock, he said. And, as I didn't drive, he offered to take us, and we left the apartment in a rush as soon as he was ready. In the brand-new rental car we got into (he had rented it while waiting for his Triumph to be repaired), I sat with my arms crossed, silent and sleepy, while he turned the car in every which way in order to get out of the tight spot in where he had parked. We sped through Paris, and

M. Polougaïevski, who always drove in a shockingly irrational and unpredictable way, directed questions of a practical nature towards his daughter, matters concerning vacation planning and weekend trips, all questions which were purposely not addressed to *us*, the main people concerned. Little Pierre, seated next to me, was looking out the window, his schoolbag on his back, and, every time we passed a tree, I pointed to it and named it in a hushed voice for his education. Soon, taken in by the game, I told him that there exist trees even more magical, tamarisks for example, cedars and palm trees, and I even described to him a whole series of tropical trees which left him awestruck, the baobab of course, with its enormous trunk, and I spread my arms to emphasize its size. Go ahead, give it a try, I said. Oh no, even bigger, I said, even bigger. Using all his strength, he stretched his arms out as far as he could. You really are a tiny little guy, I said, patting his head. M. Polougaïevski, from time to time, gave a concerned look in the rear-view mirror, and we smiled at each other in secret, little Pierre and I, in the backseat. Having reached the school past eight, we rushed through the door and entered into the deserted playground like a gust of wind, which, speed-walking, the four of us crossed at a fast pace before going into the main building. In a small glass-enclosed office sat a secretary to whom M. Polougaïevski, knocking impatiently on the windowpane, explained the reasons behind little Pierre's tardiness. The secretary looked at him through the window, appeared not to understand, and, finally getting up, opened the door and told him that he'd have to speak with the assistant principal, third office on the right at the end of the hallway. Reaching the end of the hallway without having found the assistant principal's office, M. Polougaïevski disappeared into the large cafeteria, looking for someone to question. He came back looking offended, and, giving up on trying to find it, he asked little Pierre if he could lead us to his classroom. Little Pierre led the pack, schoolbag on his back, guiding us through the school's long, brightly lit hallways, turning around from time to time to see if we were still following him. Having reached the classroom, he stopped to wait for us—here *bon-papa*, this is it, he said—and, after a rather amusing adult conversation in front of the door, we softly knocked and tiptoed in. It was a modern classroom, dominated by yellow and white colors, the walls decorated with kids' drawings, with tiny desks from behind which sat about twenty little boys and girls staring at us. The teacher got up from her desk to come greet us and, while *bon-papa*, very gentlemanly and near ready to kiss her hand, apologized with charming and diplomatic words for interrupting her class, she responded coquettishly by saying that there wasn't any problem at all and led the three of us out into the hallway, leaving the door cracked behind her to watch over the class. Here, M. Polougaïevski immediately pulled out all the stops, combining a coaxing mischievousness with the strictest sense of logic in order to explain the reasons behind little Pierre's tardiness and, before he was able to further seduce her with some Latin quotation, she apologized for having to cut short this conversation and left us to get back to her students while the three of us stood on our toes, looking through the transom, and spotted little Pierre in his class, seated in the fourth row next to a little curly-haired blonde girl in sky-blue overalls. In the playground, which we slowly walked across while chatting, M. Polougaïevski, in a great mood, asked us if we'd like to go to Créteil in order to pick up his car and the propane tank. Off we were then towards Créteil, speeding forward on the beltway, passing cars here and there with dangerous turns of the wheel. M. Polougaïevski sat hunched over the wheel as if for added speed, and, seated in the back, I watched, with a certain concern, road signs fly by indicating Nancy and Strasbourg. Fortunately we forked off towards Créteil just before the exit that would inevitably have taken us to Alsace and Lorraine and, driving around in the rain on gray streets in the new part of the city, we went off in the direction of the shopping center (now looking back on it, good God, what a day).

We spent only one night in London, in fact, Pascale and I, it's the only small complaint that I could make about England. After dinner—our first dinner together—we got back to the hotel and Pascale went straight to bed to lie down. Sitting next to her, I spoke to her in a hushed voice while tickling her forehead with my finger, and she nodded her head at times, keeping her eyes closed, imperceptibly moving her lips; then, as she was no longer responding, I realized that she had dozed off. It's true, no matter what mood she was in, I had noticed that she always had a sort of natural and fundamental languor about her, and it touched me every time to note, although at times she could be very lively, that she permanently challenged life with a lethargy that was just as remarkable. I got up and walked over to the window, where I lingered for a moment looking out. The park was dark and stretched out of view into the night. I could make out the gates down below; a taxi, from time to time, passed by silently in the street. I closed the blinds and, walking back over to the bed, I took off her jacket, gently, so as not to wake her, holding her head up flat with my hand. Then I took off her dress, which she helped me pull off by raising herself up accordingly, and I wanted to unfasten her bra, but, struggling, I thought that it would be much easier to detach it with my hands behind my back, and, sitting with my back against hers—we were back to back—I unfastened it easily, well rather easily. What a burden. I then put her things on the armchair, and was lost in thought. Pajamas, Pascale let out in a whisper. Standing in the center of the room, hands in pockets, I looked at her. Pajamas, she repeated, eyes closed, and she rolled over wearily, stretching out her arm. I took her pajamas out of her bag, sea-blue pajamas, large and ironed, with a white-edged collar, and, sitting her up in the bed, I had her put on the top; she complied, head drooping down in front of me, while I buttoned it up, right to the very last button. Light, she said, exhausted, so that someone would turn it off. She formed a kiss with her lips while scratching her little panties (goodnight, she said, and drifted off).

The next morning, I woke up, still half-asleep in the partial shade of the room, Pascale in my arms, and I was gently caressing her breasts under her pajama top. She wasn't any more awake than I was and, both of us still sleeping, we moved closer together in our sleep, hands touching cheeks or running fingers through hair, feeling around blindly, my cock in her body, still all warm from the night's rest. We slept a little longer like this, held lightly in each other's arms, with little shivers and hot chills from time to time that suggested troubled sleep. She was the first to wake, finally, opening her eyes with surprise when I ejaculated. She playfully dug her face into my cheek and smiled brightly at me, hand on my temple, whispering into my ear. The room was bathed with the shadowy light of a gray day, and we lingered for a long time under the covers, making plans while watching the rain fall. Sitting next to me, she had taken a train schedule out of her bag and was flipping through it on the bed, completely naked apart from a white sock and her reading glasses. I was looking at her, lying on my back, intrigued by the presence of this sock (what troubled me above all, in fact, was not knowing what had happened to the other one). I briefly rummaged around the end of the bed with my warm and somnolent feet and, not finding it, I leaned over the side of the bed, one hand on the ground, to check the floor. There it was, the sock, rolled up in a ball on the carpet, at equal distance between the nightstand and the television. What it was doing there?—a mystery. I mentioned this to Pascale who, looking at her feet, comparing them, noted the disparity between the two and then continued to flip through the train schedule without giving the matter any concern. The night train, she continued, imperturbable, all the while playing with her little bare toes that wiggled in the air, left late in the evening, which would give us all day to visit London (but we had to check out at noon, you know).

After having paid the young, gray-skirted, white-topped receptionist for the room, we discussed the possibility of leaving our suitcase at the hotel. Since it wasn't too cumbersome, we decided to take it with us and we left the hotel in a hurry in the rain, running alongside building fronts. We took shelter in an entryway while the downpour made itself a strong deterrent to our plans, and we stood there holding each other, hair wet, both scrutinizing the sky in opposite directions. Taking advantage of a slight lull, we went on our way, and, after having walked for a good half-hour in the rain, as we passed a large hotel I asked Pascale if she would like to stop and have a coffee, or even tea if she preferred, I was up for anything. For anything. I opened the hotel door and caught sight of a doorman in full regalia, frock coat and gray waistcoat, who, seated in a lounge chair, was taking a break in the lobby. He fixed his hair confusedly when we entered, and, standing up nonchalantly, went back to his position in front of the door, from where, hands behind his back, he began to scrutinize the horizon. I turned around to look at him, holding my bag, and Pascale, hair soaked and hanging over her eyes, continued walking forward, stretching out her arms to let her sleeves drip. We walked across the lobby and, wandering randomly through various hallways, circled around the hotel before settling down in a large room with pale yellow wallpaper, majestically complex chandeliers hanging from the ceiling, couches against the wall and coffee tables on which newspapers were nicely spread. I took a seat in a large armchair and looked around for a moment, lost in thought, my hair pasted to my head and my cheekbones wet, a drop of rain placidly sliding down towards my chin. I personally found the place delightful, there was hardly anyone there; at the back of the room, behind a tea tray, a woman was reading a detective novel with a pair of lorgnettes. We spent the whole afternoon there, stepping out of the room from time to time and leaving behind us our tray with our empty glasses and the remains of a light snack that we had for lunch. We lingered in front of shop windows in the lobby, where watches and scarves were on display. There were also shirts propped up vertically on a display table, single-colored or striped, and walking off while continuing to look absent-mindedly at other displays, we took the stairs to go visit the hotel's halls, strolling slowly through different floors (we met people at times, came across a few would-be lovers).

At the train station, arriving in the late evening, we found a luggage cart and sat down on it, side by side at the edge of the platform, our suitcase in front of us. I would get up at times, walk around the cart, and Pascale would watch me go around, slightly turning her head to follow. After having bought a few daily papers, each one forming a large, thick bundle full with various Sunday supplements, I sat back down on the cart and, sorting through the papers I had stacked in a pile next to us, I picked one up and flipped through it, found out what happened in sports over the weekend, then moved on to world politics (that's what gets me going, world politics). From time to time, people would pass by in front of us, and I would lower my paper for a moment, lost in thought, contemplating what I had just read. Other people also waited in the lobby; in front of the ticket counters or under an announcement board, a janitor stabbed thick papers with a sharp rod (we could have easily believed we were in Manchester). Pascale, seated next to me, had put on her reading glasses and was studiously reading her newspaper, taking up all the space on the cart. As our train's departure time was approaching, people began settling behind us, some with suitcases, others with backpacks placed on the ground, little yellow and orange massifs from which spewed travel maps, a pair of shoes at times, and they formed a semblance of a line following our lead, with outgrowths of luggage here and there, someone sitting on a suitcase. We were the first ones there, Pascale and I, seated on our cart in front of the platform. Finally, a ticket collector unhooked the chain and we stepped foot on the platform, leaving our cart behind us in the passageway.

We reached Newhaven in the middle of the night, and the train came to a slow stop alongside a dark and silent platform. From our compartment's window, we could make out warehouses, a few giant cranes towering over the tracks, freight cars stopped in the storage yard. Turbulent gusts of rain came down on the platform and, in the distance, I could see a multitude of drops in a beam of light coming from the maritime train station. I woke up Pascale who was sleeping in the most Pascale-like way across from me, and, gathering together the newspapers, we got off of the train and followed the other passengers. In the brightly lit entrance of the maritime train station, while people were already rushing to reach the access way to the port, Pascale went to have a seat next to the customs information counter and immediately fell back to sleep. I left her there like that for a moment, head lying on her travel bag, and walked around the entryway, hands in pockets. There were telephone booths there, display counters of shipping companies. A shop with duty-free items was closed, and I lingered a bit in front of the plate-glass window, squinting to look at the aisles inside, at shelves of bottled alcohol in the darkness. Further off in the distance, while I continued to walk around, I caught sight of a photo booth next to the custom's office, an old metal booth with a gray curtain hanging open. The floor was marked by a discolored area at the foot of the stool, with humid footprints here and there. On the exterior of the booth, in a glass frame, were some overexposed samples of the machine's previous work and a brief explanatory note giving instructions that needed to be followed in order to produce equally amazing results. I made sure that I had the necessary amount of change on me to have the pictures taken and walked into the booth, and closed the curtain behind me.

I had been sitting in the semi-darkness of the booth for a while already, stool adjusted to the appropriate height, and I felt no hurry to insert my change into the machine.

The conditions were now perfect, it seemed to me, for thinking. A few minutes earlier, on the maritime platform, I had stopped to watch the rain fall in a bright projected beam, in the exact space delineated by the light, enclosed and yet as devoid of material borders as a quavering Rothko outline, and, imagining the rain falling at this place in the world, which, carried by gusts of wind, passed through my mind, moving from the shining cone of light to the neighboring darkness without it being possible to determine the tangible limits between the light and shadows, rain seemed to me to represent the course of thought, transfixed for a second in the light and disappearing the very next second to give way to itself. For what is the act of thinking—if it's not the act of thinking about something? It's the flow of thought that is so beautiful, yes, the flow, and its murmur that travels beyond the world's clamor. Let yourself attempt to stop thought, to bring its contents to light, and you'd end up with (how could I say, how could I *not* say rather) trying to preserve the quavering, ungraspable outlines, you'd end up with nothing, water slipping through your fingers, a few graceless drops drying out in the light. It was night now in my mind, I was alone in the semi-darkness of the booth and I was thinking, protected from outer torments. The most favorable conditions for thinking, the moments when thought can let itself naturally follow its course, are precisely moments when, having temporarily given up fighting a seemingly inexhaustible reality, the tension begins to loosen little by little, all the tension accumulated in protecting yourself against the threat of injury—and I had my share of minor injuries—and that, alone in an enclosed space, alone and following the course of your thoughts in a state of growing relief, you move progressively from the struggle of living to the despair of being.

The ferry had just left Newhaven, and I could still make out in the distance the shore stippled with orange light. The sea was dark, almost black, and the sky seemed to meet it at the horizon, starless and without end. There was practically no one on the deck; behind me, two hooded silhouettes were stretched out on a bench, a wool blanket over their shoulders. I leaned forward over the ship's rail, coat collar flipped up, and I watched the ship trace its progression on the water's surface. We were irresistibly moving forward, and I felt like I was moving forward as well, splitting the sea without insisting or forcing, as if I was progressively dying, as if I was living perhaps, I didn't know, it was easy and I couldn't do anything about it, I was letting myself be carried away by the movement of the boat in the night and, watching wavelets crash against the hull with a lapping noise that had the quality of silence, its softness and its thickness, my life was moving forward, yes, in a constant renewal of identical wavelets.

The boat was progressively leaving Newhaven further in its wake, and soon all we could see in the distance was a faint line of fading colors merging with the sea. I turned back around and stayed for a moment on the deck, leaning against the guardrail. In front of me stood a metal staircase that led to the upper gangways; smoke rose up out of the boat's large funnel, a flag attached to the mast flapped in the wind. I had my hands in my coat pockets, and I felt the damp photos I had just made. They weren't completely dry yet, and my fingers slightly stuck to their surface. I took them out of my pocket and blew on them softly, then, igniting my lighter, I brought them close to the flame and examined them under the light of my lighter. They were four black and white photos, zoomed in on my face, also showing my open shirt collar and the dark shoulders of my coat. I wasn't expressing any emotion whatsoever in the photos, apart perhaps from a kind of lassitude felt from being there. Seated on a stool in the booth, I was looking straight forward, plainly, head lowered and eyes defensive—and I was smiling at the lens—well, I was smiling—that's how I smile.

Leaning over the guardrail, photos in hand, I saw the endless sea, waves swelling off into the distance, immense and foamless. The rain, which so far had not ceased its drizzle—a very light mist that mingled with the sea spray and that made clothes damp, palms clammy—suddenly began to fall violently on the deck and I walked away from the guardrail watching the sea transform into a giant black and noisy mass pummeled by the downpour. I left the deck and, after having gone down the stairs into the inside of the boat, I walked through large spaces, dark and silent, where, on each side of me, people were sleeping in the darkness on rows of beige, padded folding chairs. From time to time, someone would lift up his head and watch me walk by with curiosity, but half asleep. I kept walking before reaching the back of the boat and found myself in a big circular, silent room, with a bar closed behind a grilled metal shutter and a dark, deserted dance floor. There were close to forty people there sleeping in the room, stretched out everywhere, on chairs and on the floor, curled up in sleeping bags. Pascale was there too, and she slept like no other, my love, her little eyes closed and her head lying on her travel bag.

Later on, not having been able to sleep and having stayed there seated in the darkness with my eyes open, I left the room and walked around the hallways of the boat, here and there avoiding bodies asleep on the floors. At the corner of a landing, a little more animated than the steerage, I lingered a moment behind a man who seemed to be intensely preoccupied by an electronic machine. On the screen of the machine, aircraft carriers loaded with helicopters had to take off as fast as possible in order to sink other boats while avoiding the opposing fighter jets. Less than a meter from me, leaning over the machine, the man frantically worked the joysticks, having his helicopter suddenly gain altitude—lips pressed tight, and thrusting his pelvis against the machine—discharging a salvo of electronic beams that blew up boats one after another, up until the point where, an enemy aircraft appearing, twisting and turning and jolting back the joysticks, he lunged back almost pushing me off my feet in trying to oppose a fatal parade of shells shooting him down. The game over, he turned around to ask me if I had a light, very calmly, and I was able to note that this man had an apparently normal attitude. We even exchanged a few words in French; I asked him if he knew if there was still a bar open on the boat, and, thanking me for the light, he took a drag of his cigarette, fingers still shaking, and let me know, convulsively blinking, that in his opinion the self-service restaurant should still be open. I went down the stairs to the boat's lower deck and crossed the few meters that separated me from the restaurant. It was a dark and sordid room with a few grimy portholes rendered opaque by the night; some cafeteria furniture—Formica furniture, light beige—was bolted to the ground, with metal bars serving as armrests. Fifteen people or so were seated around the tables there, amidst dirty plates, full ashtrays and crumpled packs of cigarettes. I picked up a tray and walked down the marked line that stretched alongside the glass food displays; I then grabbed a half-bottle of Sancerre from the beverage shelf. At the register dozed an obese employee, his greasy hair all stuck together with sweat, who wore black pants and a white shirt unbuttoned to expose his sagging chest shiny from perspiration. He had an open bottle of beer next to him and, arms folded across his chest, he watched with indifference as I moved toward the register. I moved forward slowly in line, my half-bottle of Sancerre balancing on my tray, which I slid along on the rail in front of me, and, not finding any glasses, apart from the plastic cups piled up on the counter, I went to ask him if I could have a glass made of glass. A glass, you know, a good ol' glass. Why, are these not glasses? he said, pointing to the little plastic cups. I said yes, kind of, but I explained that I would prefer a real glass, if that was possible. A real glass, he said. Yes, it's much nicer, I said while distractedly scratching the table. He looked at me. You got to admit it, I said in a soft voice, you got to admit it. All right, you want a glass, is that it? he said, annoyed, getting up from his stool. Yes, a glass, I said, that didn't seem to me to be an extravagant request. A stemmed glass if you could, I added cautiously (better to be picky than embittered in life, right?).

Having taken a seat in the back of the room, I stayed there with my legs crossed, and I drank my Sancerre in a small glass mustard container adorned with smurfs that the man at the register had found for me. He had sat back down now and was sweating in silence on his stool, arms folded across his chest. A lady moved forward in line sliding her tray along the rail; a couple of middle-aged punk rockers, in the back of the room, were calmly eating sausage. I was there, yes, in the self-service restaurant of this boat headed towards Dieppe, and I had a particularly heightened awareness at this moment, as often happens when, travelling through transitory and continually ephemeral spaces, not a single known point of reference can be mentally identified. The place in which I was sitting was dissolving little by little in my consciousness and for a perfect moment, I was nowhere if not motionless in my mind, with the place I had just left slowly disappearing from my memory and that to which I was approaching still far away. I took a small sip of my Sancerre and, next to me, on an empty seat, I noticed an abandoned camera, a little black and silver Instamatic camera stuck down in a recess of the bench.

I had returned to the deck, and, in my pocket, amongst various papers, I could now feel the rigid contact of the little camera. I hadn't planned on stealing it, no. When I had picked it up, I simply had planned to give it to the man at the register, but right when I was going to hand it over, as he was busy giving back change, I turned around and left the room. Then rushing up the stairs out of fear of running into someone, I understood that there was no going back and, suddenly struck by panic in hearing some noise behind me, I started to take pictures hastily in order to finish the roll, random pictures, of stair steps and of my feet, all while running up the stairs with camera in hand, snapping and winding immediately, snapping and winding to finish the roll as fast as I could. Reaching the deck, I went to look out over the ship's rail and, while I was beginning to catch my breath, I heard one of the deck doors open behind me. I quickly hid the camera in my coat pocket and didn't move, standing still in front of the rail. A man headed towards me, passed slowly behind my back. When he had disappeared, I took the camera back out of my pocket and, pushing the little switch forward to open the body, I took out the cartridge of film, which I stowed away in my coat pocket.

The wind was picking up now, and I heard a regular scraping noise of a cord rubbing against a pulley. Clear-cut shadows intertwined around me, shadows of windlasses and launches, of stairs and of metallic gangways. Not being able to come to terms with keeping the camera, I intended to go back down to the restaurant to put it back where I had found it, then immediately leave the room trying not to attract the least bit of attention. But if by any chance I ran into the camera's owner, what explanation would I be able to give him? I didn't know. I left the deck and took care not to pass anyone on the stairs. Having reached the restaurant door, I stood flat against the wall and glanced in the room to scope out the scene. There were no more than a dozen people, for the most part silent, and nothing abnormal seemed to be going on. I entered the restaurant and picked up a tray in order to go through the line. Since I had walked in, however, I felt that the man at the register was watching me from his stool, and his eyes locked on me making me ill at ease. Hand in my coat pocket, I held the case firmly between my fingers and, not reaching a decision of whether or not to keep moving, I stayed there motionless in line, looking at the food options.

Back on deck, I headed over to a back corner of the ship, sheltered by a metal stairwell that led to upper gangways, and, taking a seat on a wooden trunk that must have contained life vests, I stayed there for a while, arms folded in the darkness, neck leaning against the cold and humid metal of the wall. The boat moved forward in the night, and I heard the purring of the motors, the sound of waves against the hull. Here and there, on the deck, were streaks of light that lit up large parallel slats of the wooden flooring. I was sitting motionless in the semi-darkness, and, in my coat pocket, I felt the camera case that jutted out against my thigh. I didn't give it back, no, I wasn't able to give it back. Before leaving the deck, I walked along the ship's rail for a few minutes and leaned to look out over the side for a moment. There was still no land in sight, the sky was immense in the night and the sea itself seemed to stretch up into the skies. Sometimes, yes, I thought of death. Looking at the waves below, I took the camera out of my pocket and, almost without moving, I let it fall overboard, smashing against the hull before bouncing off into the sea and disappearing in the current.

The dock water at the Dieppe port was almost black, dirty and lustrous, with mauve or green reflections here and there like streaks of oil. The ship berthed around five in the morning, after an infinite number of maneuvers to get it docked. It was still dark when we got off the boat, eyes sleepy and hair disheveled. Pascale took a few steps on the quay before stopping on the immense platform that stretched before us, and we watched the first trucks debark from the boat and drive off slowly, headlights lit, towards the port. In front of the main building, where the customs office and the border police were stationed, a long line of passengers formed, and, as it was practically not moving, I walked around the port while waiting for it to pick up. I walked for a rather long time in the darkness, not knowing where I was going, stopped from time to time by a fence or some gate that forced me to make a detour. Much further on, alongside the sea, I stopped a moment to watch the fisheries lit up in the night, several covered warehouses in which fish merchants bustled about, weighing wooden crates which they then put on stands, spraying down the ground, rinsing out empty containers with a small hose. Others, wearing oilskin or large pullovers, were passing back and forth through puddles with rubber boots, loading a refrigerated truck parked nearby with crates of fish. In front of the maritime port, which I could make out in the distance, the line of passengers seemed hardly to have moved, and I continued on my way, walking alongside other docks around the port. Pascale was all alone in the middle of the large platform, abandoned and fragile in the darkness. I rejoined her and we waited there still a bit longer, looking around holding hands. There was no longer anyone there. Refrigerated trucks, from time to time, left the port grounds, and we turned our heads following their departure, watching them drive off slowly on the freeway. I love you, I whispered.

Seated in front of a plate-glass window in an overheated café next to the Saint-Lazare train station, we were having breakfast, wearily stirring our spoons in our coffee glasses. It was still dark outside, and brightly lit buses, from time to time, slowly left the Cour de Rome and joined the already dense traffic on the boulevard. It had to be seven o'clock, seven fifteen, this Monday morning, and we had just arrived in Paris. The café was very lively, and the door kept swinging open, letting in abrupt and swirling drafts of cold air that made us shiver. The owner, behind the bar, served espressos to anyone who would listen to him, sliding the sugar bowl down the zinc counter. I lit up a cigarette, and, as I looked out the window, Pascale, sitting across from me with her elbows propped up on the table, looked dreamily at her croissant while fighting to not fall asleep before having finished it. I gently stroked her cheek and we gave each other a small, sleepy kiss across the table, soft and furtive, then clinked together our café au lait, cheers, and the coffee splashed up in our heavy porcelain glasses as we placed them back down on their saucers.

The premises of the driver's ed office were dark and freezing when we arrived. Pascale had closed the door behind me and grabbed my hand, without a word, looking at me tenderly in the darkness. Neither one of us moved, and for a moment we simply looked at each other in silence, softly smiling about the fact that we were together. A little lamp was lit on the desk and it was as if we were isolated on an island of green light emanating from the lampshade; the filing cabinets hardly took shape in the shade of the light, and there were a few empty seats in the darkness. In the back of the room, a whole wall was decorated with street signs of various shapes, triangular and circular, painted red and white, some yellow with black stripes, with evocative icons of railroad crossings and falling rocks, and a moose in mid-air as well, elegant and enigmatic, which I stared at for a while in the darkness. Pascale bent down to pick up the mail from under the door and, while she sorted through it, I went to look out the window; I began pensively sketching rectangles on the window with my finger, rectangles superimposed like different frames for imaginary photos, with here a very large angle delimiting in space a view of buildings side by side, there a tight framing that isolated a single car, a single person walking on the sidewalk. Then, lighting up a cigarette, I stayed there a few more minutes watching the street and went to go sit down on the floor in the back of the room. I covered my shoulders with my coat, sitting still. Against the wall underneath the projection screen, I stared at the ceiling and took a puff of my cigarette from time to time. Pascale, whom I looked at standing there next to her desk in the little island of green light, continued to open letters, filing them away in a drawer one by one as she went along. She lifted up her head a moment to think, and I looked at her affectionately, without moving, and put out my cigarette. Tonight, I stole a camera, I said quietly.

The Boeing now picked up speed on the runway and I sat still in my seat. I was letting myself be carried away by the lifting movement of the plane, trying to become one with the machine's irresistible acceleration in order to use its surge to take flight myself—and I took off very slowly, left the ground and already stabilized myself in the air above Orly while the doors of the overhead baggage compartments ceased to shake. We were flying for a half-hour already and, through the windows, I was looking at the blue and sunny sky above the clouds, a monotonous layer of clouds that looked like an ice floe below, white and solid, in no way fluffy, with contours and shapes and ridges, a stretch whose protrusions the sun softly lit up. Further on along the side, the sky continued out of sight, so intriguingly blue, so smooth, so close yet serenely distant, unfathomable and inaccessible. The plane seemed to be motionless in the air, nothing moving nearby, and, pressing my forehead up against the window, I was drowning my thoughts in these mysterious though welcoming masses of air, thinking that if I had kept the camera I would have been able to take some pictures of the sky as it is now, to frame long rectangles uniformly blue, translucent and almost transparent, capturing this transparency that I had eagerly sought out a few years earlier when I had wanted to take a photo, a single photo, something like a portrait, a self-portrait perhaps, but without me and without anyone, only a presence, full and stripped bare, painful and simple, without a background and almost without light. And, continuing to stare at the sky, I realized now that I had taken this photo on the boat, that I had suddenly and successfully extracted it from me and from the moment, running up the boat's stairs in the night, practically unaware of being in the process of taking photos and yet ridding myself of this photo I had so long yearned for; I immediately understood that I had seized it in the fleeting intensity of life, though it be inextricably buried in the inaccessible depths of my being. It was like a photo of the feverish impetus that I carried in me, and yet it already testified to the impossibility that would follow, to the disaster that it would create. For I would be seen fleeing in the photo, I would be fleeing as fast as I could, my feet leaping the steps, my moving legs flying over metal gaps between the boat steps, the photo would be blurry but still, the movement would be frozen, nothing would move, not my presence nor my absence, there would be the whole stretch of stillness that precedes life and that that follows it, hardly more distant than the sky out onto which I was looking.

I flew back to Paris the next night, a bit fatigued from moving from one place to another, from these continual comings and goings. It was already dark in Orly when I left the airport, and I took a taxi driven by a silent lady with her dog who was sleeping on a cushion at her side as we drove off on the highway in the night. Lights on the dashboard shined in the semi-darkness, and rapid streaks of headlights lit up the inside of the taxi from time to time. We passed from one lane to another, and I noticed a shimmering of light at the horizon, little flecks of variegated brightness that were scintillating in the night. After a few kilometers, the lady turned off towards a gas station to fill up the tank, and I got out to smoke a cigarette in the parking area. In the distance, I could see Orly-Sud buildings lit up, flashing red lights of planes slowly descending towards the runway. Later in the night, I wandered for a long time around the streets of Paris, and I went down the stairs that lead to banks of the Seine. It was very dark, and the river flowed silently in the murky night. I was there, yes, back in Paris, and, standing up along the Seine in the black shadow of a solitary linden tree, I was looking at the surface of the water in the night thinking about the camera that I had tossed into the sea, and I pictured it somewhere there in the English Channel, accumulating rust right now forty meters deep, surrounded by dark and opaque water, slightly leaning back on the sea floor with some frayed seawood stuck to the case.

In the following days, I went to have the pictures developed, which I had taken on the boat. In the little clear blue envelope that was given back to me, there were eleven negatives in color, the loud colors of pictures taken with an Instamatic, a man and a woman, the man young and corpulent, in his thirties, blond and pale skin, and the woman a little younger, short blonde hair, wearing a red top in most of the negatives. These faces weren't at all familiar to me and I had no recollection of having seen them, but I couldn't question the fact that the camera must have belonged to them, the last picture had indeed been taken in the boat's self-service restaurant, probably right before the camera had been forgotten on the seat. Not a single picture that I had taken myself had turned out, not one, and, looking carefully over the negatives, I realized that after the twelfth photo, the film was uniformly underexposed, with here and there a few undefined shadows like imperceptible traces of my absence.

There wasn't a single light in the distance, only a deserted road that continued off into the night, with some undergrowth flanking the sides, a large farm at the horizon, and I was walking all alone alongside the road, no longer able to make out behind me the gardens of the property from where I had just left. Before leaving, my hosts had offered to drive me to the train station, but I had preferred to walk and I had left immediately in the night, walking around the perimeter of the wooded park on their property. Beyond the fence, the road stretched out of sight in the darkness, a very narrow road that appeared to be never-ending. There wasn't a sound around me, if not for the regular noise of my feet stepping on the ground, and I kept walking forward alongside this abandoned road looking at the three-quarter moon, with a little oblong cloud passing slowly through its halo. The first dwellings of a village were soon in sight, and I crossed the main street, deserted and shutdown, with rows of silent houses and closed businesses, a dry-goods store and a café with dark windows from behind which I could make out the shadows of chairs stacked on tables in the backroom. The train station was located a bit outside the village, and I stopped at the small square in front of the building, with a flowered roundabout and a *monument aux morts* standing tall in the semi-darkness. A few streetlights dimly lit up the surroundings, and there wasn't a soul in sight, not even a car, only a few stripes of white paint on the blacktop that formed deserted parking places. All was silent. The train station's facade was slightly granular and looked like a stage décor, with its little inlaid clock that read quarter till midnight.

When I entered the station, I found myself in a deserted room with wooden benches against the walls and a glass door through which I could make out the platform in the darkness. There wasn't anyone at the ticket counter, and the adjoining office, in which there were red lights blinking on a control panel, was equally uninhabited. A newspaper was open in the back of the office, with a pair of glasses lying flat on the pages. I went out onto the platform, walked down it a bit in the night and, not finding anyone, apart from a frightened chicken fleeing across the tracks, I left the station to have a look around.

I went back to wait in the train station and, sitting on a wooden bench against the wall, I sat there patiently, flipping through the pictures that I'd taken out of the clear blue envelope. I had already looked at them several times since the previous night, these eleven colored pictures finely framed by a white border, and I had begun little by little to familiarize myself with the unknown faces of the camera's owners. The man was by himself in only one picture, in some kind of large park in the rain in which, sporting a yellow cagoule, he stood, head lowered, at the edge of a fountain. In all the other pictures, the young lady appeared alone, in London or alongside a British road, at times in a pea coat standing in front of a building or in a pink top seated behind a plastic coffee cup in a museum café. In one of the last pictures, they were photographed together in front of the fence of a public building, and the man had his arm around the young lady's waist, both smiling self-consciously at the camera. What disturbed me in these seemingly anodyne pictures, besides the fact that I was being confronted with an intimacy to which I should never have had access, was a sense of involuntary indecency that these pictures expressed. Even the nature of the negatives, for the most part botched-up and taken at random, gave them the appearance of having an incontestable reality, a brutal and almost obscene reality that forcefully imposed itself on me. But what disturbed me even more, flipping through the whole series again, was one I looked at closely. It was the next to last in the series, and up till then I hadn't noticed anything. The picture was taken in the large lobby of the maritime train station in Newhaven and I suddenly realized that, behind the young lady standing in the foreground, you could make out the edges of the customs information counter, next to which clearly appeared Pascale's sleepy silhouette.

I was still all alone in the train station, and it wasn't until a little after midnight that an employee showed up, blue blazer slung over his shoulder. I got up to follow him when he went into his office and, asking him questions across the ticket counter while putting the pictures back into the envelope, he told me that the last train for Paris had left and that the next was at seven o'clock the next morning. He turned off the light in his office, then in the whole room, flipping a switch that controlled all the lights of the station, and, leaving his office, he went to close the door that opened out onto the platforms and invited me not to hang around too much longer in the train station, he had to lock it up for the night. I waited next to him while he bolted the main door and he hardly responded to my questions, didn't know if there were still Paris-bound trains leaving from Orléans. Then, curtly returning my wave, he took off and I watched him drive away slowly in the night on his moped. I wasn't planning on going back to my host's place at this hour, and I left the station following the direction that he had taken, ended up leaving the village and soon found myself at the intersection of a busy national highway, along which I began walking in the direction of Orléans. I was walking on the narrow shoulder, alongside a little roadside ditch in which dark water stagnated, and car headlights blinded me every couple of minutes. At times heavy loads passed by at full speed in the night, and the blast of air that they left behind them shook the surroundings in their wake. I was trying to keep myself at a distance from the edge of the road and ended up cutting across a supermarket's parking lot. I walked there in the darkness to meet back up with the road and, amongst iron scraps and empty beer bottles that littered the muddy grass of a flower bed, I caught sight of a daisy, all white and trembling, lit up intermittently by the headlights of passing cars. Little by little, there was less traffic on the freeway and I ended up in a completely deserted zone, with no longer a single light in the distance, without homes and with no trace of industrial activity, only immense stretches of fields on either side of the road. I had no idea how far I had walked and I was coming up on a crossroad that branched off deep into the countryside when I saw a road sign in the night indicating that Orléans was seventeen kilometers away.

It was an extremely normal crossroad (four streets that connected in a deserted plain, with a phone booth in the semi-darkness, the door slightly cracked) and there was nothing around, the countryside was perfectly dark and silent. Ominous clouds in the sky had partially covered the moon, thick clouds whose cotton edges could be made out in the near-hidden halo of the moon. Rummaging through my pockets on the edge of the road, I realized that I had only one coin and, crossing the deserted roadway, I entered the phone booth and lit my lighter to look on the glass walls for the booth's telephone number. It was almost two in the morning and, the phone in my hand, I was unsure whether or not I should dial Pascale's number. I had put my coin in the machine, and the dial tone continued to amplify in the dark while I waited. I closed my eyes for a second and, slowly, very slowly, I pushed the buttons to dial Pascale's number, and soon started to hear the first rings resonate in the profound darkness of the booth. Then I heard someone pick up and, in the most complete darkness, my ear and my hand fragilely pressed against the earpiece, I heard in the night her sleepy voice.

I had asked Pascale to call me back at the booth, and I stepped out for a second into the fresh air, walked around a bit in the night with my eyes on this phone booth that was going to ring for me any minute now. It stood there dimly in the night, gray, almost silver in the moonlight, and there was no light on the horizon, only fields that stretched out of sight into darkness. I went to sit down on the edge of the road and, as time passed and as Pascale had not yet called me back, I came to wonder if she had not fallen back asleep. I ended up returning to the booth and, closing the door behind me, I let myself slide slowly down against the wall and sat on the ground. My pants legs scrunched up to expose my socks and, seated flat on the floor, I looked through the window at the deserted countryside in the night. Cars drove by at times, whose harsh lights lit up my face when they passed the cross-road, then nothing would be left in the darkness but a streak of headlights that I would watch slowly disappear in the night.

Seated in the darkness of the booth, my coat wrapped around me, I didn't move. I thought. Yes, I was thinking and, when I was thinking, eyes closed and body sheltered, I imagined another life, identical to this life in shape and scope, its breathing and its rhythm, a life in every way comparable to *life*, but with no wounds imaginable, no aggression, and no possible pain, far away, a detached life that blossomed up through the thinning ruins of exterior reality, and where a different reality, interior and peaceful, accounted for the sweetness of each passing moment, and it was scarcely words that appeared to me then, nor images, few sounds apart from the same familiar murmur, but moving forms that followed their course in my mind like the movement of time itself, in the same infinite and serene predictable way, trembling forms with undefined edges that I let silently flow in me in a calm and sweet flux, purposeless and grandiose. I was thinking, yes, and grace would be forever renewed, fears silenced, terrors vanished, and it reached the point where even in my mind painful traces of possible attacks were starting to dissolve. Hours passed in an unvarying sweetness and my thoughts continued to maintain amongst themselves a network of sensual and fluid relationships, as if they were continuously adhering to a play of mysterious and complex forces that would come at times and stabilize them into an almost palpable point of my mind and at other times would have them fight a moment against the current to return immediately to their infinite course in the peaceful, silent state of my mind.

Morning was approaching now, I was watching it rise up through the glass walls of the booth, it was still dark, but a darkness softened by the clear and blue-streaked dawn, nothing was moving in the neighboring countryside, and the day was slowly rising before my eyes, coating little by little the surrounding sky with soft and luminous tints that gave the atmosphere a fragile and transparent brightness, and, sitting looking out through the glass walls of this telephone booth, completely isolated in the deserted countryside, I watched the day rise and simply thought of the present, of the present moment, trying to fix in my mind once again its fleeting grace—as with the tip of a needle one immobilizes the moving body of a living butterfly.

Living.

Towards an Infinitesimal Novel

Interview with Jean-Philippe Toussaint
by Laurent Demoulin

The following interview was conducted by Laurent Demoulin and was published as an afterword to the second edition of the French novel Camera *(Editions de Minuit, 2007). It is published here with the permission of the author and of the Editions de Minuit.*

Laurent Demoulin: Would you say that *The Bathroom* (1985) was successful as a novel in France, whereas *Camera* (1989) established the success of a writer? Several critics, who were disappointed in *Monsieur*, said *Camera* confirmed an author's talent.

Jean-Philippe Toussaint: This excluded, at any rate, the idea that I had written only one book. There is a continuity between *The Bathroom* and *Camera*, of course. Something rather usual happened with *Monsieur*, a common phenomenon called "the second, failed novel," as though everyone was content to say, "The second novel is always less good." Which is, to be honest, not impossible. But I was not aware of this possibility when *Camera* came out.

LD: Given the success of *Camera*, did you think you could now live from your writing?

JPT: I have never thought of this in economic terms. The tough moment was rather before the publication of *The Bathroom*: I felt I'd become a writer but had no publisher. Afterwards, I never thought about it, I wrote, and that was it. I was completely immersed in the action, and wasn't reflecting upon the action. I wasn't aware, either, of how my books fit into the literary landscape.

LD: Critics, as well as the first academic theses, which date back to when *Camera* was published, put the focus mainly on the philosophical nature of *Camera*. So the spotlight was put on the intellectual aspect of your work, not on the humoristic one. Wasn't this a rather dangerous emphasis?

JPT: No, quite the contrary. Back then, people who didn't like my books accused me of being a light, offhanded, trendy author who lacked depth. It was therefore a blessing in disguise that critics focused on the philosophical aspect of the book, on the reflections it develops about thought and photography: it balanced everything out, as it were. *Camera* is indeed both a very serious and very casual book. My books never display a great unbalance between the mundane and the intellectual, or between the provocative, I-couldn't-give-a-damn attitude of *Camera's* narrator on the one hand, and the philosophical and metaphysical reflections on thought and the passage of time on the other.

LD: There is a significant rupture in the tone of the book at one point: the first part is humorous, and then the novel shifts to a state of anguish, and becomes both more philosophical and more poetic.

JPT: That's right. After the boat trip the tone changes and a certain poetic solemnity emerges. It was the first time a darker tone appeared in my books, without being a counterpoint to humor, without the offhandedness of *The Bathroom* that offset the serious reflection on the passage of time.

LD: However, although the solemnity of *The Bathroom* is minimized by irony and humor, the character in *Cam-*

era is going through less of a crisis than the character in *The Bathroom*. The last few pages of *Camera* are slightly darker, gloomier, but the tragedy is played down.

JPT: Yes, it's true, *The Bathroom* can be described as the description of a crisis, whereas *Camera* is more the description of a condition, the condition of someone's place in the world. The book progressively shifts from the "struggle of living" to the "despair of being."

LD: These quotes from the book are very striking. Is it possible to read it as a reflection on the contemporary world, which relies on the struggle of living as a means of avoiding the despair of being, preferring stress to anguish? The narrator avoids stress thanks to thought, but does not avoid a profound anguish. Is this in response to the general, current mood of the world?

JPT: In my mind, that sentence clearly indicates how the book is split into two parts: the first part is dedicated to the struggle of living, which is always a great humorous device. "There's nothing funnier than unhappiness," said one of Beckett's characters in *Endgame*. Then the second part deals with the despair of being, which has to do with the human condition, philosophy, metaphysics . . . From then on, the tone is more melancholic.

LD: *Camera* is probably your most self-referential book . . . The first sentence, for instance, is almost a manifesto.

JPT: Yes, you're right, it's a manifesto, a program. I don't know how aware of this I was. But still, it took me over a month to write the first paragraph. I still know it by heart. "It was at about the same time in my life, a calm life in which ordinarily nothing happened, that two events coincided, events that, taken separately, were of hardly any interest, and that, considered together, were unfortunately not connected in any way." It's a very radical opening, and it really is having fun with the readers. Here I am, a thirty-year-old writer saying: "What I'm about to tell you is absolutely irrelevant." In other words: "I'm about to make you feel foolish." It's a very impertinent opening. I'm responding very offhandedly to Kafka's famous aphorism: "In the fight between you and the world, back the world," with "In the fight between you and reality, be discouraging." So yes, it's a manifesto, but it isn't a theoretical essay or piece; it's there, in the book itself, in the opening paragraph of the book, as a theory in action. Underlying my novel is, although it isn't expressed theoretically, an idea of literature focused on the insignificant, on the banal, on the mundane, the "not interesting," the "not edifying," on lulls in time, on marginal events, which are usually excluded from literature and are not dealt with in books.

LD: The mechanisms that you created in *The Bathroom* are perfected in *Camera*. Could we say that *Camera* is the outcome of *The Bathroom*?

JPT: You could, but *Camera* is also a dead end. It can be seen as the outcome of *The Bathroom*, but the outcome may be less interesting than the initial moment, the first attempt, the moment when a style, a manner of things, something new, appears, without our knowing quite where it comes from or how it was done. At any rate, I didn't pursue this further. Something ends with *Camera*. I opened a path and then I stopped, went on to something else, I made movies, experienced other things in my books, I thought I wouldn't write a novel like *Camera* every two or three years, but maybe others will. As far as I'm concerned, I intend to go further, I want to discover something else, find the initial impetus which had motivated me to write in the first place, a sharpness, something Kafkaesque or Dostoyevskian. My next book, *La Réticence* (1991), was written entirely in response to *Camera*. Critics had talked a lot about how light and virtuoso *Camera* was; I wanted to move away from such virtuosity, I wanted to break it apart. *La Réticence* is a difficult, demanding, tough book, it's harsh and sometimes unpolished. I wrote this book trying to keep in mind a secret guideline, a Beckettian one, the one that says: "badly seen, badly expressed," and I tried to fail to see things and to fail to say them (and I succeeded in doing so, I must say, if the reaction of the media and readers is any indication). It's the only book of mine that didn't sell, the only one that got negative reviews, but I'm very proud to have got to the end of it. *La Réticence* is the book that was the hardest to write.

LD: One striking feature of *Camera*, compared to *The Bathroom*, is the length and flexibility of the sentences.

Whereas sentences in *The Bathroom* were quite restrained, they become more ample, more stylistically daring in *Camera*. From this point of view, *Camera* is the foretelling of the long periods of time found in *Making Love* (2002) or *Fuir* [Running Away] (2005).

JPT: When I wrote *Camera*, I was more experienced, I was more at ease, stylistically speaking. I felt tense in *The Bathroom*: my sentences are short, solid. In *Camera*, I allowed myself to write longer sentences, which is much more difficult stylistically. *Camera* is both the outcome of *The Bathroom*, and a novel which announces the novels that follow, some of which were books I wrote fifteen years later; a lot of elements are set in motion in *Camera* which have results only in *Making Love* or *Fuir*. I must absolutely stress the continuity in my work, even though I pay constant attention to the idea of renewal, even though I try very hard not to write the same book twice, even though writing is always searching. I don't think that I moved on to something different after *Making Love* or *Fuir*, not at all, everything already existed in embryo, was potentially present, there in the first books. In this respect, the third part of *Camera* is very revealing, for it contains a lot of elements one finds in *Making Love* or *Fuir*: melancholy, poetic solemnity, the theme of the night, longer sentences, rain, metaphysics, and even light: the description of rain falling, seen through the rays of a streetlight, could have been a scene in *Making Love* or *Fuir*.

LD: Critics started seeing you as a leader when *Camera* was published. In the French magazine *Le Point*, Jacques-Pierre Amette even uses the term "standard bearer."

JPT: Back then I had no idea what was at stake in this. The one who was aware of it was my publisher, Jérôme Lindon. He could see that a new generation of writers was emerging and he knew how useful it would be to create a new literary movement, which could succeed the *Nouveau Roman*.

LD: The media also started talking about a "school" back then. The piece in *Le Point* was entitled "The nouveau 'nouveau roman.'" Other expressions were coined: "the minimalist novel," "the Minuit school," "the postmodern novel," "the impassive novel."

JPT: There were several phrases going around, but none of them took on. That was the context in which Lindon asked me, one day, if I knew what this new literary movement could be called. Back then, I had dodged the question, but now, eighteen years later, I think I can answer it. It took me quite some time, about twenty years of reflection, but I found the answer. The answer is in the last words of *Making Love*, where I'm writing about an infinitesimal disaster. I didn't write "infinitesimal" thinking of a theory, but I didn't write this word lightly either. Infinitesimal is the response, and I suggest speaking of "the infinitesimal novel." The problem with the idea of the "minimalist novel" is that it's very simplistic. The term "minimalist" calls to mind the infinitely small, whereas "infinitesimal" evokes the infinitely large as much as the infinitely small: it contains the two extremes that should always be found in my books.

SELECTED DALKEY ARCHIVE PAPERBACKS

Petros Abatzoglou, *What Does Mrs. Freeman Want?*
Pierre Albert-Birot, *Grabinoulor.*
Yuz Aleshkovsky, *Kangaroo.*
Felipe Alfau, *Chromos.*
Locos.
Ivan Ângelo, *The Celebration.*
The Tower of Glass.
David Antin, *Talking.*
António Lobo Antunes, *Knowledge of Hell.*
Alain Arias-Misson, *Theatre of Incest.*
John Ashbery and James Schuyler, *A Nest of Ninnies.*
Djuna Barnes, *Ladies Almanack.*
Ryder.
John Barth, *LETTERS.*
Sabbatical.
Donald Barthelme, *The King.*
Paradise.
Svetislav Basara, *Chinese Letter.*
Mark Binelli, *Sacco and Vanzetti Must Die!*
Andrei Bitov, *Pushkin House.*
Louis Paul Boon, *Chapel Road.*
Summer in Termuren.
Roger Boylan, *Killoyle.*
Ignácio de Loyola Brandão, *Teeth under the Sun.*
Zero.
Bonnie Bremser, *Troia: Mexican Memoirs.*
Christine Brooke-Rose, *Amalgamemnon.*
Brigid Brophy, *In Transit.*
Meredith Brosnan, *Mr. Dynamite.*
Gerald L. Bruns,
Modern Poetry and the Idea of Language.
Evgeny Bunimovich and J. Kates, eds.,
Contemporary Russian Poetry: An Anthology.
Gabrielle Burton, *Heartbreak Hotel.*
Michel Butor, *Degrees.*
Mobile.
Portrait of the Artist as a Young Ape.
G. Cabrera Infante, *Infante's Inferno.*
Three Trapped Tigers.
Julieta Campos, *The Fear of Losing Eurydice.*
Anne Carson, *Eros the Bittersweet.*
Camilo José Cela, *Christ versus Arizona.*
The Family of Pascual Duarte.
The Hive.
Louis-Ferdinand Céline, *Castle to Castle.*
Conversations with Professor Y.
London Bridge.
North.
Rigadoon.
Hugo Charteris, *The Tide Is Right.*
Jerome Charyn, *The Tar Baby.*
Marc Cholodenko, *Mordechai Schamz.*
Emily Holmes Coleman, *The Shutter of Snow.*
Robert Coover, *A Night at the Movies.*
Stanley Crawford, *Log of the S.S. The Mrs Unguentine.*
Some Instructions to My Wife.
Robert Creeley, *Collected Prose.*
René Crevel, *Putting My Foot in It.*
Ralph Cusack, *Cadenza.*
Susan Daitch, *L.C.*
Storytown.
Nicholas Delbanco, *The Count of Concord.*
Nigel Dennis, *Cards of Identity.*
Peter Dimock,
A Short Rhetoric for Leaving the Family.
Ariel Dorfman, *Konfidenz.*
Coleman Dowell, *The Houses of Children.*
Island People.
Too Much Flesh and Jabez.
Arkadii Dragomoshchenko, *Dust.*
Rikki Ducornet, *The Complete Butcher's Tales.*
The Fountains of Neptune.
The Jade Cabinet.
The One Marvelous Thing.
Phosphor in Dreamland.
The Stain.
The Word "Desire."
William Eastlake, *The Bamboo Bed.*
Castle Keep.
Lyric of the Circle Heart.
Jean Echenoz, *Chopin's Move.*
Stanley Elkin, *A Bad Man.*
Boswell: A Modern Comedy.
Criers and Kibitzers, Kibitzers and Criers.
The Dick Gibson Show.
The Franchiser.
George Mills.
The Living End.
The MacGuffin.
The Magic Kingdom.
Mrs. Ted Bliss.
The Rabbi of Lud.
Van Gogh's Room at Arles.
Annie Ernaux, *Cleaned Out.*
Lauren Fairbanks, *Muzzle Thyself.*
Sister Carrie.
Leslie A. Fiedler, *Love and Death in the American Novel.*
Gustave Flaubert, *Bouvard and Pécuchet.*
Kass Fleisher, *Talking out of School.*
Ford Madox Ford, *The March of Literature.*
Jon Fosse, *Melancholy.*
Max Frisch, *I'm Not Stiller.*
Man in the Holocene.
Carlos Fuentes, *Christopher Unborn.*
Distant Relations.
Terra Nostra.
Where the Air Is Clear.
Janice Galloway, *Foreign Parts.*
The Trick Is to Keep Breathing.
William H. Gass, *Cartesian Sonata and Other Novellas.*
A Temple of Texts.
The Tunnel.
Willie Masters' Lonesome Wife.
Etienne Gilson, *The Arts of the Beautiful.*
Forms and Substances in the Arts.
C. S. Giscombe, *Giscome Road.*
Here.
Prairie Style.
Douglas Glover, *Bad News of the Heart.*
The Enamoured Knight.
Witold Gombrowicz, *A Kind of Testament.*
Karen Elizabeth Gordon, *The Red Shoes.*
Georgi Gospodinov, *Natural Novel.*
Juan Goytisolo, *Count Julian.*
Makbara.
Marks of Identity.
Patrick Grainville, *The Cave of Heaven.*
Henry Green, *Blindness.*
Concluding.
Doting.
Nothing.
Jiří Gruša, *The Questionnaire.*
Gabriel Gudding, *Rhode Island Notebook.*
John Hawkes, *Whistlejacket.*
Aidan Higgins, *A Bestiary.*
Bornholm Night-Ferry.
Flotsam and Jetsam.
Langrishe, Go Down.
Scenes from a Receding Past.
Windy Arbours.
Aldous Huxley, *Antic Hay.*
Crome Yellow.
Point Counter Point.
Those Barren Leaves.
Time Must Have a Stop.
Mikhail Iossel and Jeff Parker, eds., *Amerika: Contemporary Russians View the United States.*
Gert Jonke, *Geometric Regional Novel.*
Homage to Czerny.
Jacques Jouet, *Mountain R.*
Hugh Kenner, *The Counterfeiters.*
Flaubert, Joyce and Beckett: The Stoic Comedians.
Joyce's Voices.
Danilo Kiš, *Garden, Ashes.*
A Tomb for Boris Davidovich.
Anita Konkka, *A Fool's Paradise.*
George Konrád, *The City Builder.*
Tadeusz Konwicki, *A Minor Apocalypse.*
The Polish Complex.
Menis Koumandareas, *Koula.*
Elaine Kraf, *The Princess of 72nd Street.*
Jim Krusoe, *Iceland.*
Ewa Kuryluk, *Century 21.*
Eric Laurrent, *Do Not Touch.*
Violette Leduc, *La Bâtarde.*
Deborah Levy, *Billy and Girl.*
Pillow Talk in Europe and Other Places.
José Lezama Lima, *Paradiso.*
Rosa Liksom, *Dark Paradise.*
Osman Lins, *Avalovara.*
The Queen of the Prisons of Greece.
Alf Mac Lochlainn, *The Corpus in the Library.*
Out of Focus.
Ron Loewinsohn, *Magnetic Field(s).*
Brian Lynch, *The Winner of Sorrow.*
D. Keith Mano, *Take Five.*
Micheline Aharonian Marcom, *The Mirror in the Well.*
Ben Marcus, *The Age of Wire and String.*
Wallace Markfield, *Teitlebaum's Window.*
To an Early Grave.
David Markson, *Reader's Block.*
Springer's Progress.
Wittgenstein's Mistress.
Carole Maso, *AVA.*
Ladislav Matejka and Krystyna Pomorska, eds.,
Readings in Russian Poetics: Formalist and Structuralist Views.

SELECTED DALKEY ARCHIVE PAPERBACKS

Harry Mathews,
The Case of the Persevering Maltese: Collected Essays.
Cigarettes.
The Conversions.
The Human Country: New and Collected Stories.
The Journalist.
My Life in CIA.
Singular Pleasures.
The Sinking of the Odradek Stadium.
Tlooth.
20 Lines a Day.
Robert L. McLaughlin, ed.,
Innovations: An Anthology of Modern & Contemporary Fiction.
Herman Melville, *The Confidence-Man.*
Amanda Michalopoulou, *I'd Like.*
Steven Millhauser, *The Barnum Museum.*
In the Penny Arcade.
Ralph J. Mills, Jr., *Essays on Poetry.*
Olive Moore, *Spleen.*
Nicholas Mosley, *Accident.*
Assassins.
Catastrophe Practice.
Children of Darkness and Light.
Experience and Religion.
The Hesperides Tree.
Hopeful Monsters.
Imago Bird.
Impossible Object.
Inventing God.
Judith.
Look at the Dark.
Natalie Natalia.
Serpent.
Time at War.
The Uses of Slime Mould: Essays of Four Decades.
Warren Motte,
Fables of the Novel: French Fiction since 1990.
Fiction Now: The French Novel in the 21st Century.
Oulipo: A Primer of Potential Literature.
Yves Navarre, *Our Share of Time.*
Sweet Tooth.
Dorothy Nelson, *In Night's City.*
Tar and Feathers.
Wilfrido D. Nolledo, *But for the Lovers.*
Flann O'Brien, *At Swim-Two-Birds.*
At War.
The Best of Myles.
The Dalkey Archive.
Further Cuttings.
The Hard Life.
The Poor Mouth.
The Third Policeman.
Claude Ollier, *The Mise-en-Scène.*
Patrik Ouředník, *Europeana.*
Fernando del Paso, *Palinuro of Mexico.*
Robert Pinget, *The Inquisitory.*
Mahu or The Material.
Trio.
Raymond Queneau, *The Last Days.*
Odile.
Pierrot Mon Ami.
Saint Glinglin.
Ann Quin, *Berg.*
Passages.
Three.
Tripticks.
Ishmael Reed, *The Free-Lance Pallbearers.*
The Last Days of Louisiana Red.
Reckless Eyeballing.
The Terrible Threes.
The Terrible Twos.
Yellow Back Radio Broke-Down.
Jean Ricardou, *Place Names.*
Rainer Maria Rilke,
The Notebooks of Malte Laurids Brigge.
Julián Ríos, *Larva: A Midsummer Night's Babel.*
Poundemonium.
Augusto Roa Bastos, *I the Supreme.*
Olivier Rolin, *Hotel Crystal.*
Jacques Roubaud, *The Great Fire of London.*
Hortense in Exile.
Hortense Is Abducted.
The Plurality of Worlds of Lewis.
The Princess Hoppy.
The Form of a City Changes Faster, Alas, Than the Human Heart.
Some Thing Black.
Leon S. Roudiez, *French Fiction Revisited.*
Vedrana Rudan, *Night.*
Lydie Salvayre, *The Company of Ghosts.*
Everyday Life.
The Lecture.
The Power of Flies.
Luis Rafael Sánchez, *Macho Camacho's Beat.*
Severo Sarduy, *Cobra & Maitreya.*
Nathalie Sarraute, *Do You Hear Them?*
Martereau.
The Planetarium.
Arno Schmidt, *Collected Stories.*
Nobodaddy's Children.
Christine Schutt, *Nightwork.*
Gail Scott, *My Paris.*
June Akers Seese,
Is This What Other Women Feel Too?
What Waiting Really Means.
Aurelie Sheehan, *Jack Kerouac Is Pregnant.*
Viktor Shklovsky, *Knight's Move.*
A Sentimental Journey: Memoirs 1917–1922.
Energy of Delusion: A Book on Plot.
Literature and Cinematography.
Theory of Prose.
Third Factory.
Zoo, or Letters Not about Love.
Josef Škvorecký,
The Engineer of Human Souls.
Claude Simon, *The Invitation.*
Gilbert Sorrentino, *Aberration of Starlight.*
Blue Pastoral.
Crystal Vision.
Imaginative Qualities of Actual Things.
Mulligan Stew.
Pack of Lies.
Red the Fiend.
The Sky Changes.
Something Said.
Splendide-Hôtel.
Steelwork.
Under the Shadow.
W. M. Spackman, *The Complete Fiction.*
Gertrude Stein, *Lucy Church Amiably.*
The Making of Americans.
A Novel of Thank You.
Piotr Szewc, *Annihilation.*
Stefan Themerson, *Hobson's Island.*
The Mystery of the Sardine.
Tom Harris.
Jean-Philippe Toussaint, *The Bathroom.*
Camera.
Monsieur.
Television.
Dumitru Tsepeneag, *Pigeon Post.*
Vain Art of the Fugue.
Esther Tusquets, *Stranded.*
Dubravka Ugresic, *Lend Me Your Character.*
Thank You for Not Reading.
Mati Unt, *Diary of a Blood Donor.*
Things in the Night.
Álvaro Uribe and Olivia Sears, eds.,
The Best of Contemporary Mexican Fiction.
Eloy Urroz, *The Obstacles.*
Luisa Valenzuela, *He Who Searches.*
Paul Verhaeghen, *Omega Minor.*
Marja-Liisa Vartio, *The Parson's Widow.*
Boris Vian, *Heartsnatcher.*
Austryn Wainhouse, *Hedyphagetica.*
Paul West, *Words for a Deaf Daughter & Gala.*
Curtis White, *America's Magic Mountain.*
The Idea of Home.
Memories of My Father Watching TV.
Monstrous Possibility: An Invitation to Literary Politics.
Requiem.
Diane Williams, *Excitability: Selected Stories.*
Romancer Erector.
Douglas Woolf, *Wall to Wall.*
Ya! & John-Juan.
Jay Wright, *Polynomials and Pollen.*
The Presentable Art of Reading Absence.
Philip Wylie, *Generation of Vipers.*
Marguerite Young, *Angel in the Forest.*
Miss MacIntosh, My Darling.
REYoung, *Unbabbling.*
Zoran Živković, *Hidden Camera.*
Louis Zukofsky, *Collected Fiction.*
Scott Zwiren, *God Head.*

FOR A FULL LIST OF PUBLICATIONS, VISIT:
www.dalkeyarchive.com